THE BLIND CONTESSA'S
NEW MACHINE

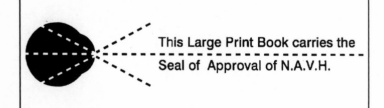

This Large Print Book carries the
Seal of Approval of N.A.V.H.

THE BLIND CONTESSA'S NEW MACHINE

CAREY WALLACE

THORNDIKE PRESS
A part of Gale, Cengage Learning

GALE
CENGAGE Learning™

Detroit • New York • San Francisco • New Haven, Conn • Waterville, Maine • London

GALE
CENGAGE Learning

Copyright © Carey Wallace, 2010.
Excerpt from "Elegy" from *Collected Poems* 1957–1982 by Wendell Berry.
Thorndike Press, a part of Gale, Cengage Learning.

Thorndike Press® Large Print Basic.
The text of this Large Print edition is unabridged.
Other aspects of the book may vary from the original edition.
Set in 16 pt. Plantin.

LIBRARY OF CONGRESS CATALOGING-IN-PUBLICATION DATA

Wallace, Carey, 1974–
    The blind contessa's new machine / by Carey Wallace.
      p. cm. — (Thorndike Press large print basic)
    ISBN-13: 978-1-4104-3067-0
    ISBN-10: 1-4104-3067-7
    1. Blind women—Fiction. 2. Inventors—Fiction. 3. Italy—History—19th century—Fiction. 4. Large type books. I. Title.
    PS3623.A44295B57 2010b
    813'.6—dc22   2010026703

Published in 2010 by arrangement with Viking, a member of Penguin Group (USA) Inc.

Printed in the United States of America
1 2 3 4 5 6 7 14 13 12 11 10

for my mother:
your trip to Italy

Until morning comes say of
the blind bird:
His feet are netted with darkness,
or he flies
His heart's distance in the darkness
of his eyes.
— Wendell Berry, "Elegy"

On the day Contessa Carolina Fantoni was married, only one other living person knew that she was going blind, and he was not her groom.

This was not because she had failed to warn them.

"I am going blind," she had blurted to her mother, in the welcome dimness of the family coach, her eyes still bright with tears from the searing winter sun. By this time, her peripheral vision was already gone. Carolina could feel her mother take her hand, but she had to turn to see her face. When she did, her mother kissed her, her own eyes full of pity.

"I have been in love, too," she said, and looked away.

"Papa," Carolina had said.

Her father had laid his magnifying glass down on the map unrolled before him. A

mournful sea monster loomed below the lens. Although it was the middle of the day, the blindness shrouded the bookshelves that rose behind him in false dusk. Only the large window over his head and the desk itself were still bright and clear.

"Nonna was blind when she died," Carolina said.

Her father nodded. "And for years before that," he said. "But I only half believed it. It was like she had another pair of eyes hidden in a box. She knew everything."

"Did she ever tell you how it happened?" Carolina asked.

Her father shook his head. "I was very young then."

"I think maybe I am going blind," Carolina told him.

Her father frowned. After considering this for a moment, he waved his hand before his face. When her eyes followed it, he broke into a wide grin.

"Ah, but you haven't yet!" he said.

She had told Pietro in the garden, when her mother had left them alone for a few moments under a sky full of stars that Carolina could snuff out or call back into existence simply by turning her head.

Pietro had laughed and laughed.

"What are you going to tell me next?" he had asked her, between kisses. "I suppose you can fly as well? And turn into a cat?"

"Already I can't see things," she insisted. "Around the edges."

"Next you will tell me you have forgotten how to kiss," Pietro said, and kissed her again.

In those first days, Carolina measured her losses by the size of her lake. Her father had dammed a length of the small river that wandered their property as a present to her mother on their fifth anniversary. But as an amateur in these things, he had only clumsily dredged the surrounding marsh. The resulting body of water, thirty paces long and half again as wide, was in no place deep enough for a man to stand fully submerged. His young wife, still homesick for the sea, had tramped loyally across the soggy ground with him on the day of her anniversary but never returned voluntarily, so when Carolina turned seven, her father had scattered stone benches on the grassy shore, filled the lake's surface with lantern-lit boats, and made a new present of it to his daughter.

This time it was received gratefully, with an appreciation that manifested, in its early days, as tyranny: already Carolina had developed a passion for solitude, and from the date of her seventh birthday demanded that she be allowed to visit the lake, which sat half a mile from the house through vine-choked pines, entirely unaccompanied. After all, she argued, what else could it mean to own something?

Completely overthrown by this reasoning, her father agreed, despite her mother's misgivings, which, from long years of disregard, had finally gone to ground and begun to emerge again as sleeplessness, forgetfulness, and truly unspeakable fears.

From this point, it became Carolina's daily habit to walk to the lake, now silver with rain, now black, now gray, now solid ice, clear or milky depending on how quickly a freeze had taken it. In her tenth year, winter's arrival had been both swift and brutal, so that the frozen lake retained an eerie clarity that allowed Carolina to see all the way to the bottom in most places, laying bare her watery property's mysteries: the sunken branches, the green weeds, the fishes' bare, bowl-shaped nests, and the deeper channel of the dammed river's original path. With a broom borrowed from the kitchen maid to sweep the snow away, Carolina spent hours in her surveying, her face red and lips blue when she arrived at that winter's dinners.

That spring, her mother had insisted her father build Carolina some kind of shelter on the banks, and he had erected a one-room cottage of unpainted wood, stained red, a few strides from the water. Light poured into it through glass windows set in all four walls. A collection of worn rugs covered the floor. The furniture was sparse: an old couch weighed down with patched velvet quilts, a desk, and a chair. The room was small. Standing in the middle of it, his arms outstretched, Carolina's father could almost touch both walls. A fireplace opened at the foot of a slim chimney behind a screen worked with brass mermaids, another of her father's well-intentioned but unsuccessful presents to her mother, who found all reminders of the sea not a comfort but a grief.

Once the cottage was built, the great house lost its grip on Carolina completely. She passed more of the nights of her remaining childhood on the couch at her cottage than in her own bed, buried like a black-eyed field mouse in piles of thick velvet, or naked in the warmth the summer sun left as a remembrance after it set. On warm nights, she threw the windows open and tacked fine scarves over them to foil the insects. Outside, the frogs and birds sang their boasts, hopes, and threats.

Because she had first learned the lake with a child's eyes, Carolina was able to believe for a while that the fact that she could no longer take it in with a single glance was just another of the many tricks her body had played on her in the mysterious operation of turning her into a young woman. The church, and the distance to the city, and the grand ballroom's once-endless expanse had all shrunk as she grew up. Why should the lake be any different?

But just after her eighteenth birthday, around the time she and Pietro were engaged, the trouble with focus at the borders of her vision advanced. She could no longer recognize figures at a dance until she turned to face them directly. At the same time, her sight contracted, as if some unseen spirit had cupped his hands on either side of her head, blotting out her sight to the right and left. The rest was lost in darkness.

Turri, of course, had understood immediately. He had raised his own hands to either side of his face. "Like this?" he asked.

Carolina nodded.

For an instant, his blue eyes widened with worry. Then they changed. He still looked

14

directly into her face, but his focus was on something far beyond her, his mind casting through the books of an invisible library. Carolina hated this expression: sometimes it passed in an instant, but often it meant she had lost him to his thoughts for the afternoon.

For the moment, however, he was still gathering evidence. "For how long?" he asked.

"Half a year," she said. "Since before Christmas."

Beyond the silk pinned in the lake house windows, a summer loon sang a few notes, then lapsed back into thought.

"I've read about it," Turri said. "Blindness can come from the sides, or from the center."

"The center?" Carolina repeated.

"Like an eclipse, in the center of your vision. But it's permanent. And the darkness grows from there."

"But in my case, it is collapsing from the outside," she said.

"That is the other kind."

Tears sprang to Carolina's eyes. She allowed them to cloud her vision, grateful for a blindness she could wipe away with a flick of her wrist. When the tears passed, Turri sat gazing at her as if she were a new problem in math.

"How long?" she asked.

"I'm sure it is different in every case."

When she didn't look away, he dropped his gaze. "I can find out," he said.

"Thank you."

"Have you told Pietro?" he asked.

She nodded.

Turri studied her for a moment longer, then gave a short laugh. "But he doesn't know."

She shook her head.

Turri took her hand.

For once, she let him.

Carolina and Turri had met for the first time when she was six and he was sixteen. Her mother had decided that spring that Carolina was old enough to attend her father's lemon blossom dance, which he held each year when his wax-leaved groves burst into bloom, to mark his gratitude to the new spring sun, the saints, or whatever gods might still be lurking in the old hills. Carolina had been allowed to pick the fabric for her own dress: a robin's egg brocade trimmed with white lace from the exotic and impossibly distant Switzerland. She spent a dozen afternoons in the seamstress's studio, where the air was thick with glimmering

16

dust motes and the scent of lily and basil that drifted in from the room next door, where the maids arranged the flowers they'd cut in the yard. As Carolina watched, the patient old woman cut the fabric for the bodice and the small bell of the skirt, then stitched the miniature gown to life, the needle in her crooked fingers drawing the thread through the folds so quickly that Carolina sometimes lost sight of it.

When the gown was complete, three days before the party, Carolina worried that she might die of joy. The old woman hung it on her wardrobe, where it shone in the morning sun like a piece of the sky. For those three nights, Carolina slept only fitfully. Often, she crept out of bed to make certain by touch that the gown was still there and that she was not being misinformed by her dreams, as so often happened. Although she had stood for a number of uncomplaining hours while the dress was measured and fitted, she refused to try it on after it was finished, half saving it as she might carry a sweet drop in her pocket until the end of the day, and half terrified of the unknowable but unquestionably profound change that would take place in her the moment she put it on.

Only an hour after the party had begun,

however, she found herself pressed against the wall in her parents' ballroom, forgotten. The air was hot and cloying with the scent of a thousand lemon blossoms, branches her father's men had pruned that day to keep the old trees healthy and force more fruit from them. Far above her head, her parents' friends exclaimed greetings and gossiped like chickens. A few had taken her hand and remarked how pretty she looked as they came in. Some of them had even dared to pat her head. But now she was lost amid an unfriendly sea of whispering skirts and legs.

Then a pair of the legs came to a stop in front of her.

Carolina threw her head back.

A tall boy with light brown hair and bright blue eyes looked her over for a moment. Then, to her shock, he took a seat beside her on the ballroom's highly polished parquet floor without making any provisions to protect his fine black trousers. With him seated and her standing, their faces were at approximately the same level. The young man did not address her.

Carolina thought hard. "Are you tired of dancing?" she asked after a moment.

"I'm not good enough at dancing to have gotten tired of it," the young man said.

His manner was earnest enough to satisfy Carolina, and his logic appealed to her despite the fact that his meaning was difficult to grasp. She nodded gravely.

The young man gazed out at the swirling crowd. "What do you think of this party?" he asked.

For a moment, Carolina cast about in her mind for a worldly lie, but her excitement over the truth quickly overcame her. "This is my first dance," she confided, watching him closely for the reaction a fact of such weight demanded.

She was not disappointed. The young man's eyes grew wide. He nodded slowly, taking her announcement in as if, as she suspected, it changed everything.

Then a movement in the crowd caught his attention. Carolina followed his gaze up to the face of a determined girl in a lavender dress, pushing through the crush of guests a few paces away. She was looking for something. This didn't seem out of the ordinary to Carolina, but it frightened the young man. He shrank back against the wall. When it didn't give way behind him, he glanced at Carolina for help. Carolina's brows drew together as she stared back, trying to understand his problem so she would know what to offer him.

Then the young man seemed to come to his senses. He scrambled to his feet.

Carolina tilted her face to see him at his full height.

He executed a handsome bow. "You look lovely tonight," he told her. "Just like you fell out of the sky." He lifted her small hand, bent low to kiss it, and slipped away into the crowd.

Carolina watched him go. Then she darted between a small forest of trouser legs suffused in a cloud of spicy cigar smoke and wound her way through the crowd at the buffet of cakes and sweets. Just beyond them, her mother's enormous crystal bowl presided over the corner table, filled with tart lemonade. A handful of yellow slices turned lazily on its surface. There, she caught sight of the young man again. The girl in the lavender dress was leading him to the dance floor by the hand.

Forgetting her gown for the moment, Carolina ducked under the heavy folds of cloth that covered the table. She emerged beside Renato, an ancient servant with a nose like a piece of melted marzipan who, she had also recently discovered, had the talent of twisting handfuls of clover into flowered crowns.

"Renato," she demanded, pointing. "Who

is that, being led around like a bad dog?"

Renato followed the line of her little finger. Then he laughed with the gentle exasperation grown people usually reserved for a child who couldn't be expected to know better.

"That's young Turri," he told her.

The small dam her father had built to stem the original river stood on the far side of Carolina's lake. Just beyond the dam, the river became a clear rocky creek that ducked into the forest and flowed on to Turri's land, emerging to become the flashing ribbon at the foot of the Turris' back garden. The Turri home itself sat just out of sight over the next hill, facing the same dusty gold road as her father's house.

This made Turri one of Carolina's closest neighbors, and after their first meeting she recognized him from time to time on the road as he went by. Apart from the lake, her favorite place was an alcove window on the second floor of her father's house, where she was a close observer of the neighborhood traffic. Each figure that passed on the road had a role in a complicated ongoing drama she constructed from whatever details she could glean about them on any given day. Turri was a favorite character in these scenes. In stark contrast to the end-less parade of placid old women carrying their unvarying baskets of lemons and eggs, he gawked at the clouds and stumbled over rocks. He chased flying things with his hat. He came to abrupt halts for no reason at all. In addition, he was likely to be in pos-session of any number of evocative props: a pair of brown mice in a wire cage; a thick candle that sparked and steamed, but didn't go out in the rain; a basket of feathers that the wind caught and scattered just as he disappeared over the rise, giving the effect that some enchantment had transformed him into the flyaway plumes.

But they didn't speak again until Carolina was ten, when she discovered him standing in the hard sun on the side of that same road, glaring down at what seemed to be a tangle of women's dresses and sticks, embel-lished here and there by lengths of the same twine she'd seen the gardener use to tie sweet peas to their leafy towers.

Carolina had been engaged that day in her own explorations. It had recently come to her attention that many of the things adults had told her about the world were not true. Her mother was rarely tired, as she claimed: it was just that she preferred spending her days in her own rooms to speaking with

Carolina or her father. This realization led Carolina to begin testing other claims. She unleashed an entire stream of overheard curses at a stand of undeserving daffodils and discovered that her tongue did not, in fact, turn black. She slept with a coin her father had given her under her pillow for a week, then carried it carefully to the lake and threw it in, but a swan boat did not emerge from the rings inside of rings that spread on the dark water, as she had wished.

As a result, Carolina had decided to test the limits of her more immediate surroundings. She knew that the road led over the hill to the Turri villa, which she had passed a hundred times. But in the opposite direction, the path forked. One branch led to the small town she sometimes visited with her mother to buy books or cloth. The other turned into her father's forest, but their carriage had never gone down it in Carolina's memory. From the carriage window, she could only catch a short glimpse of treetops brushing over a shady lane. Then the mysterious road turned sharply and vanished in the woods.

"Where does it go?" Carolina had asked a few weeks before, holding back the carriage's thick curtains.

"Nowhere, darling," her mother had told

her. "It may have gone to the river once. There's nothing there now."

This answer only inflamed Carolina's suspicions. Carolina's mother had told her there was nothing in the old gardener's shed, but on investigation, Carolina had discovered that it was crammed with treasure: jars full of colored glass, brown paper packets decorated with drawings of flowers and vegetables, enough burlap to make a wedding dress, and spiderwebs spun so large they could catch a child.

Determined to see for herself where the road led, Carolina struck out across her father's lawn and tramped through the forest that claimed that corner of his property, using a system she had developed for not walking in circles in the woods, a fate she knew often befell less clever travelers. Quite simply, she walked from tree to tree, always choosing one slightly to the east, which was where she judged that the road must run. But despite her new system and some admirable self-control in resisting the blandishments of a number of intriguing flowers that beckoned from beyond her chosen path, she emerged from the brambles still in sight of her own gate.

Her disappointment was interrupted almost immediately by the sight of Turri and

24

his machine.

"What does it do?" she called, picking her way through the stubble of yearling trees that had bravely taken root in the parched grass between the road and the forest.

Turri glanced up at her for a moment and then resumed glaring at the wreckage. "It's a trap for angels," he said.

Before Carolina could decide whether this was a joke, a lie, or some new category, the pile of silk and sticks burst into flames.

For one long breath, pale blue and gold fire swept over the delicate folds, caressing the cloth without consuming it. Then the sticks began to crack, and the twine charred and curled.

Carolina leapt onto the pile, stamping madly. After just a few measures of her strange dance, the fire was vanquished. She stood in the ruins of the machine, the ghost of the fire rising as faint smoke around her bare knees, and looked at Turri.

He looked back at her with the sudden keen interest of a scientist whose specimen has been unwise enough to reveal some extraordinary trait: a bird repeating the name he had mumbled in his sleep, a mouse struggling to rise on two feet, a fish that lights up as the sun drops into the sea.

Troubled by his gaze, Carolina extracted

herself from the wreckage. "I hope I didn't break anything," she said, retreating into politeness in this completely unmapped territory.

Turri laughed.

Carolina's eyes narrowed. The inexplicable laughter of adults always filled her with rage.

At the change in her expression, Turri composed himself immediately. "I'm not laughing at you," he said. "I wouldn't dare. You might strike me with lightning."

With this, he knelt and began to roll the remains of his experiment into a bundle, as thick as a man and nearly as tall. When he rose to his feet he pulled it with him, propping it upright in the road. The jumble of sticks and fabrics gave the overall effect of a beloved scarecrow, brightly adorned for burial.

He seemed slightly surprised to discover that Carolina had not disappeared from the scene. "Do I know your name?" he asked.

"Carolina," she said.

"Carolina," he repeated. Then he tilted his head with all the dignity of one grown man acknowledging a debt to another. "Thank you."

Carolina tilted her head in return.

As Turri turned away, she stepped back into the shade. Nothing broke the silence of the bright afternoon except the crunch of Turri's boots. A strip of turquoise silk, escaped from the bundle, trailed in the road, raising a thin plume of golden dust behind him.

Turri, when the time to marry came, had been widely considered an unsuitable husband by the girls his age. For years, he had tormented them with his questions, pranks, and inventions. Most famously, he had trapped a pair of local beauties in the upper reaches of a plane tree for the better part of a day when the primitive pulley elevator they were helping him test failed under the weight of two strapping young men who had hoped to join them in the seclusion of the leaves. As the girls told it, they had only barely survived the ordeal. While Turri worked feverishly to replace the broken boards and repair the twisted mechanism, the lunch hour passed. Now dizzy from hunger, the girls had survived only by catching the wild apples and handkerchief full of cherries their suitors heroically tossed to them in the high branches.

This was the stuff of legend, but Turri also had a string of lesser crimes to his name. For Loretta Ricci's fifteenth birthday, he had created strange black candles that burned with green flame. They were the sensation of the evening, until they began to stutter and spark, singeing the hair and dresses of half a dozen young ladies before a resourceful maid drowned the remaining tapers in the punch. He had taught Contessa Santini's bird to count to one hundred, after which the creature became so proud he refused to sing. Contessa Santini, unable to bear the bird's constant tally of each second of her life, finally threw the window open and shook the poor thing out of its cage, condemning it to a freedom in which, everyone agreed, its intellectual accomplishments could not be expected to protect it from the wind and the rain. Worse, Turri had no discernible ambition, and beautiful manners that he chose to use only as the spirit moved him, making his frequent social blunders all the more unforgivable.

But young women's warm hearts can forgive far more than rude words, and while these were the reasons the girls whispered among themselves or presented tearfully to their parents, the roots of their reluctance to marry Turri sprang from a hundred smaller impressions that the girls themselves could barely name, in part because they were hardly worth mentioning. Sometimes his eyes lit up when speaking with a girl, not at a tender revelation or a witty turn of phrase, but with curiosity about a crystal in her jewelry, or an exotic flower in a nearby vase. His face often remained blank as everyone around him burst into laughter. Most unnerving, he often seemed to hang on a girl's every word only to reveal under questioning, just moments later, that he hadn't heard a thing.

And though he couldn't seem to hold the thread of conversation in polite society, when a girl, by pure coincidence, stumbled on a subject that was of interest to him, she was lost for the evening. He was capable of ruining an entire dance, talking for hours about salt mines, constellations, metallurgy, lizards, with the innocent confidence of a child convinced that everyone else found the world as strange and fascinating as he did.

This posed a problem for Turri's parents, but not one the family was unfamiliar with. The Turri line was known for producing two distinct kinds of men. The majority were careful stewards who had turned the Turri lands into some of the richest in the region through judicious innovation and a remarkable talent for numbers. Turri's father was a prime specimen of this type: well-respected despite his noticeable shyness, he personally inspected his vast plantings of grain instead of leaving the task in the hands of overseers, and was also responsible for upgrading and expanding the meticulously planned irrigation system his grandfather had introduced to the property half a century before.

But in a memorable minority of Turri men, this bent toward innovation produced full-blown dreamers of the very worst sort: those with the energy, resources, and intellect to inflict their fancies on the rest of the world. These were the Turri ancestors who had cut a quarter mile of terraces into the hill the Turri home stood on, leading all the way down to the river at its foot, and who, in a later generation, had designed the most elaborate waterworks the area had ever seen, not to provide for any crops, but to draw water from the river up to the top of the hill, so it could cascade down the terraces to the river again. These dreamers tore up fields of wheat to plant saffron or rubber trees, stabled their horses side by side with peacocks and llamas, and even convinced one of Carolina's patient forebears to allow apples, plums, and even a spray of roses to be grafted into the branches of his innocent lemon trees. But Turri, his father's only child, had the worst case of this malady the Turri line had ever produced, and the nearby families could see it.

So his parents were forced to strike a bargain. Like Turri, Sophia Conti came from a good home, and she was undeniably pretty. But her mother had been an invalid since Sophia was a child, and there was no denying that she had grown up wild. Even before the boys her age paid her any mind, she preferred the company of men, hovering behind her father's chair as he and his friends argued the merits of their favorite horses or shouted about politics. Although her father ignored her caresses and the childish thoughts she whispered to him, she discovered that her pretty smile quickly won her the affection of many of the other men, who petted her when she stopped at their knee. By the time she blossomed into womanhood, she was well acquainted with the mind of a man and how to manage it. At just fourteen, she was rumored to be the reason for Regina Mancini's broken engagement, when the Mancini family could no longer turn a blind eye to the flagrant public attentions Regina's fiancé paid Sophia. There was no way for Sophia to emerge from the scandal unscathed. To marry the man would have been an admission that she had encouraged his defection from Regina. But her refusal of his desperate entreaties branded her, even at that tender age, as a dangerous creature, lacking the natural respect a young woman should hold for the sacred bond of marriage.

Not that Sophia made any attempts to correct this impression. If anything, her command over men grew more complete after the incident. They thronged her at parties and scuffled when they met at her door to pay their respects. At any given time, half a dozen of them claimed to be her favorite, presenting various trinkets as proof of her devotion: a lace handkerchief, a crushed flower, black ribbon. But twice as many stories also circulated about her indiscretions. She disappeared with men onto rooftops and into closets. She emerged from the trees with them, her jewelry askew. By the time she was seventeen, she had received nine sincere proposals, but none of them had survived the scrutiny of the families of the young men in question.

Completely unsuited for each other, Turri and Sophia were also each other's only hope for a suitable match within their small circle. Their union was practical and abrupt: they married within weeks of their fathers' negotiations, when Turri was twenty-five and Sophia twenty. Her child, Antonio, was born less than a year later, and the question of whether he was also Turri's son was widely, and almost openly, debated.

But there was no question of Turri's devotion to the boy. Even before the child was old enough to walk, neighbors were surprised to discover Turri carrying him on his shoulders along the side of the road or tramping down the riverbank, expounding seriously on new thinking on theology or modern controversies about the stars.

"He wanted to bring Antonio," Sophia joked bitterly at a party the year after her son's birth. "But he has only taught him Latin yet, not how to dance."

Unsurprisingly, when Antonio did begin to speak, he was a strange child. His first word was *pomegranate;* his second, *telescope;* and to his mother's chagrin, he didn't speak her name until months after he began to say *Papa,* a word he applied indiscriminately to Turri, his nurse, the gardener, the groom and stable boy, as well as the huge flocks of crows that settled from time to time on the lawns that surrounded the Turri villa.

Carolina was sixteen and Turri had been married for less than a year when she emerged from her lake house on a cold spring morning to discover him standing at

33

the water's edge. His back was to her. On the lake, clouds of the mist that rose from the water in the night towered over his head.

Barefoot on the top step, Carolina pulled the velvet blanket closer around her shoulders. The door behind her clattered shut.

Turri twirled, eyes blazing.

The sight of her seemed to throw him off balance. He staggered a few steps on the dewy grass before he regained his footing. When he did, he was laughing.

"I thought you were a bear," he said. "My plan was to smash your nose with that rock." He pointed to a small gray stone on the bank, worn smooth and forgotten by the river.

"It's not very big," Carolina said doubtfully.

"Bears have extremely sensitive noses," Turri told her. "It's your one weakness. My other guess was that you were a gigantic insect. On some southern islands they have butterflies the size of eagles."

"But this is Italy," Carolina said.

"I had forgotten that," said Turri. "I was trying to think how to capture you without destroying your wings."

"But where would you keep a creature that size?"

"In my laboratory," Turri said without

hesitation. "In a frame stretched with a mosquito net, hung from the ceiling."

Carolina considered this for a moment. Then she hit on another problem. "What do butterflies eat?" she asked.

"It would never come to that," Turri said. "I'd build the frame and put you in it. You'd turn around once and flap your wings unhappily, and I'd climb right back up, give you my arm for a perch, and carry you to the window to set you free."

Carolina's stomach dropped as she imagined the long fall from the top story of the Turri house, before her phantom wings caught her and carried her up.

Turri shrugged. "But chances are there's no such thing. You can't believe everything you read. The old drunks who first surveyed America claimed the lakes in Virginia were full of mermaids."

As he said this, he glanced at her lake with something suspiciously like hope. The white mist brooded over the water, impenetrable.

"I'm sorry," he said when he looked back. "I've intruded." The flame of his story extinguished, he suddenly seemed much younger to Carolina. His face was pale, his eyes unnaturally bright, the skin below them blue, like a man who hasn't slept all night.

A wave of pity rolled through her.

"My father says it's impossible for a neighbor to intrude," she said gently.

Turri took in the curves of her body and the angles of her elbows under the velvet with something more than the desire she had begun to recognize in the eyes of the older boys. He followed the lines of her figure as if they obscured a secret, some meaning inscribed by an unseen hand, if he could only read it. Then his gaze returned to her eyes.

Carolina lowered them in confusion.

"That's very kind of you," he said.

Turri took her at her word. From that day, he was a regular visitor to the lake. Even when their paths didn't cross, he left traces. Most often, she found his footprints in the mud on the banks, but some days she arrived in the first hours of the morning to find coals still orange in the ash of her fireplace. Sometimes he had rearranged this or that: he might lay several pens in a neat row on her desk, all their sharp nibs pointing west, or push a china doll into the arms of a glass monkey, so that they seemed to dance. Now and then they met when Turri wandered out on a twilight walk, or surprised her sleeping in her boat as it drifted

36

on the black water through a humid afternoon.

He was curious about everything, and his curiosity was flattering. Carolina had discovered already that people rarely wanted answers to the questions they asked, but eventually she realized that, on the subjects that interested him, Turri would listen almost indefinitely, interrupting only to ask another question. He wanted to know about lemons: how long the blossoms held to the branch; the time it took a bud to grow to fruit; any strange shapes the fruit might take; and whether she had seen these oddities or just heard of them. He was curious about the fish and the birds, which were already half tame because of Carolina's habit of carrying a napkin full of bread with her to scatter when she arrived. The fish in particular were beggars. Whenever they caught sight of a human shadow on the water, they crowded together at the boat landing and waited for bread to fall from the sky.

"Look at that," Turri said. "I wonder if you could train them?" He threw a shred of a leaf onto the water. It landed on the heart of his own shadow and turned there for a moment before one of the fish, small but quick, darted up to claim it.

"To do what?" Carolina asked.

"Swim in formation," Turri said. "Jump in arches."

Safe below the surface, the fish tasted its prize. Disappointed, it released the scrap. The unwanted leaf dropped slowly through the water and disappeared into the gloom that shrouded the bottom of the lake.

At the end of that summer, Turri began to court a bold red sparrow who, judging by the depth of color in his still-perfect feathers, might have been too young to know better. Turri's technique was simple. The birds were already accustomed to snatching up bits of bread from Carolina's feet, and in the course of a single day, they grew used to Turri and his crumbs as well. Then Turri began to sit on the grass at the water's edge, scattering the crumbs incrementally closer and closer to him. More conservative birds took flight each time the crumbs moved toward Turri, but the brightest one matched him inch for inch, finally pecking a bit of crust from Turri's open palm. By September, the sparrow would land on his hand, and when Turri was absent, Carolina sometimes believed she glimpsed the bird hopping from twig to twig, whistling impatiently, with all the heart-pricked irritation of a lover who has been made to wait.

"Do you think he'll remember us next year?" Carolina asked.

"I don't know," Turri said. The bird was perched on the slope of the back of his hand, pecking experimentally at one of his knuckles. "This kind is supposed to be impossible to tame."

For her part, Carolina treated Turri something like the fish and the birds: part of the perfectly familiar but ever-changing landscape of her lake. If she found him on the bank when she awoke, she was liable to greet him briefly and then retreat back into the house to sleep or read for another hour. She sometimes climbed into her boat and pushed out onto the water in the middle of one of his stories, or fell asleep while he was explaining something, as if his voice were not much more than the sound of wind in the leaves, pleasant but unimportant. When he was gone for a spread of days, she might wonder about him for a moment, but she didn't miss him and he played no part in her dreams.

Those, at the moment, were filled with Pietro, the only son of the distinguished family whose lands lay upriver from Carolina's lake, bordering her father's property. Pietro's mother had died during the birth of his younger sister, when he was only five. At that time, his father's oft-noted long silences had become permanent, and his neighbors would have happily arrived at the diagnosis of madness due to grief had he not continued to produce wines of such excellent quality. His stubborn insistence on retaining his claim on such a small corner of reality, while he seemed to bid the rest of it to ride merrily on to hell, agitated people. The idea of a sane mind working on among them in silence for years without ever revealing itself frightened some and infuriated others. In retaliation, they both pitied and spoiled his son.

Pietro was invited to every child's party, every wedding, baptism, and confirmation, and later, every dance and most dinners. Even as a boy, he was handsome: taller than the other children by a few inches and later by an entire head, with dark curls over dark eyes and a fine mouth most often spread in an easy laugh. He had a weakness for marzipan, so the maids were asked to make the treat for his visits even when it was not Christmas or Easter. A song he praised would be requested by someone at every event for the rest of the season. Caught up by both Pietro's charisma and the general competition among the local boys to outdo one another in catering to him, one of his young friends, on receiving a magnificent colt as a birthday present, actually insisted that Pietro be the first to ride the animal around the courtyard, instead of him.

Pietro's delight in these things was infectious, and his gratitude outsized. With perfect sincerity, he told every family in the area that their maid made unquestionably the best pastries for miles. After taking the first ride on his friend's new colt, he declared it the finest animal in Italy. All the mothers he spoke with understood him like no one else, all the boys he knew were brave, all the girls he met were pretty, and all the men he knew were wise. With this charm, and with a carelessness about his own person that stemmed perhaps from the lack of a mother's warning hand, or perhaps from his father's inattention, he easily rose to leadership among the boys his age. He was always the first to climb a tree, peer into a window, wade across the river, or ride a kidnapped mare out of a neighbor's stable on any given escapade.

Among the girls, of course, he was an object of devotion more fervently worshipped than any of the cold statues of the saints. A girl could live for weeks on a single glance from him. His small compliments

and offhand remarks formed a new scrip-
ture, and in breathless conversations and
lonely, dream-drunk nights they built whole
theologies from them. Any real attention
paid to one girl — two dances in an evening,
a flower broken from a bush to decorate her
dress — was liable to elicit tears or bitter
jealousy from the others, and in one case, a
fit of fainting, although Pietro seemed blissfully unaware of the reason for the scuffle
even as the unfortunate girl's father and
brother carried her from the party. He
thereby revealed a lack of self-consciousness
about his own powers that only further
endeared him to both the ladies and his
friends.

Pietro was only seventeen when his father
was found dead one morning among his
long rows of beloved vines. Relatives took in
Pietro's younger sister and married her off
a few years later to a bookish military man
in a seaside capital. But Pietro, the named
heir although too young to inherit, remained
at the ancestral home under the care of family servants who had long since given up all
pretense of trying to turn him from any path
he chose. Of course, the natural result was
a string of conquests among the local maids
and small farmers' daughters. But Pietro
never took advantage of girls from the bet-

ter families, with a delicacy of class feeling that their fathers could look on with nothing but approbation. Among young ladies of his own circle, Pietro was a perfect gentleman, so full of respect that the girls despaired.

Carolina's fascination with Pietro, at the outset, was little more than a symptom of her age. At sixteen, her notion of love was largely a dream: secrets confided in the shelter of rose gardens, letters pinned to young trees, rescue from roadside bandits. For this purpose, from a distance, Pietro was the perfect cipher. No other boy was as tall as him, or as handsome. Unlike the other boys, he never looked uncertain, or childish, or worried that the horse he was riding might slip from his command and bolt for the stables. No other boy had run toward the fire that consumed half of the Rossi granary one icy winter night, instead of away from it.

The summer that Turri began to visit her lake, when she was sixteen, Carolina had no reason to believe that she was a favorite with Pietro. But she had several well-worn bits of hope. Pietro knew her name. He had asked her to dance at a party the previous year, and several parties later, when he finally asked her again, he still remembered it. He had complimented her dress at a garden lunch. This season, he had taken the opportunity at a baptism to ask Carolina if she would like some punch. When she said yes, he returned with a glass and spoke with her for several minutes about his opinions on children, which he believed to be both angels and demons, trapped together under the same new skin.

Carolina's fresh young heart could not resist. From that moment on, she was another devotee of his: at parties, she watched his every move and lost her breath if their eyes met. The memory of a smile from him, carefully hoarded, could make her heart race for days. He stood proudly at the center of all her fragmentary plans, returning to her from some as yet undeclared war, riding on a black horse over fields of foreign snow; striding toward her down a row of vines, a bunch of dark grapes in each hand; standing beside her at the threshold of a great ballroom, her hand in his as a servant recited their names, a momentary hush fell, and the curious crowd turned as one to regard them.

But despite the purity of her devotion to Pietro, her parents frowned on Turri's visits to the lake. A month or so after Turri's first appearance there, Carolina's father discovered the pair of them standing together on the bank. Turri was testing a theory of his about the number of rings that formed on still water, throwing pebbles through the mirrored surface while Carolina counted for him. Carolina's father emerged from the woods about fifteen paces from them. When she caught sight of him, Carolina turned and waved. Then she realized that she had lost her count of the black and silver rings.

"I'm sorry," she said to Turri. Turri glanced up, a white pebble between two fingers.

"It's all right," he said. "We have more pebbles."

Her father strode across the river grass lawn between the forest and the lake.

"Hello, Papa!" Carolina said. She closed the distance between them, threw her arms around his neck, and kissed his cheek above his dark beard. It wasn't a surprise to her to meet him. Every few weeks he visited the lake in the course of his aimless rambles, perhaps spurred by the same restlessness that had driven Carolina through the forest since she was a child: not the disease of a true explorer but a nobleman's lazy curiosity, easily satisfied by a tour of the property that confined him.

Her father kissed her cheek in return. Then he looked at Turri with evident displeasure. "Turri," he said, in greeting.

Turri grinned, transferred the cache of pebbles from his right hand to his left, and extended his right hand in welcome. "This is a pleasant surprise," he said, taking so little notice of her father's coldness that Carolina wondered briefly if it had actually escaped him.

After a pronounced pause, Carolina's father extended his own hand. The two of them shook.

"Welcome to our humble experiment," Turri said.

"We're investigating fluid dynamics," Carolina explained, linking her arm through her father's. Her father covered her hand completely with his.

"A rock never makes more than a dozen rings, no matter how hard you throw it," Carolina told him. "They just get wider and wider until they disappear into the reeds."

"And I suppose this discovery will cure cholera," her father said.

Turri laughed and nodded, as if the older man had made a good joke at his expense.

Carolina squeezed her father's arm, silently protesting his coldness. "But if you watch for another second," she continued, "sometimes the wave bounces off the bank and all the rings begin to collapse." This small mystery was her favorite part of the day's experiment. "Show him," she told Turri.

Turri opened his hand to select one of the white pebbles.

"Oh, no," Carolina's father said. "I'm not a man of science. The sun rises and sets. I don't ask it why."

Turri's fingers curled slowly back over the pebbles, like a flower closing for the night.

"Your mother is asking for you," Carolina's father told her. This was not only a lie, but such an improbable one that Carolina glanced at him in astonishment.

For the first time, Turri seemed embarrassed. "Please, don't let me keep you," he said.

"You understand," Carolina's father said, as if this were an order.

Turri nodded.

"You are welcome to stay until the experiment is finished," Carolina's father told Turri, as he led his daughter away.

Carolina and her father walked in silence through the sun-shot forest. When they reached the main house, he released her arm with no further mention of her mother's request. But that evening, her mother sent a servant to summon her.

Her mother's rooms were on the second floor of the house, overlooking the forest that hid Carolina's lake. As always after dark, candles glimmered from every corner. A candelabra lit the pages of the romance her mother closed as Carolina entered. Half a dozen other dark wax columns flickered on the vanity, the bookcase, the table beside the bed. Carolina's mother was in her favorite spot, on the divan by the window.

Carolina paused in the doorway, uncertain. Her mother rarely invited Carolina to her room, and as a result Carolina never came on her own. Carolina often begged a bundle of cheese and bread from the cook on her way to the lake, and her mother preferred to take meals alone, so it was possible for the two of them to go without speaking for days. As a child, Carolina had peppered her mother with questions, since her mother rarely spoke unless asked directly. But as Carolina grew, the questions she wanted to ask became more difficult to put into words, until the problem of saying what she meant finally baffled her into silence. Now their exchanges were marked mostly by long pauses punctuated by unimportant observations. But for Carolina, her mother still held the force of an oracle, and whether she believed her mother's statements or not, she worried them in her mind as if they were a divine riddle.

Her mother patted the cushion beside her. Obediently, Carolina crossed the room and sat. The window she now faced was black. Orange candlelight wavered on the uneven glass.

Her mother settled back. "How is the lake today?" she asked.

"It's pretty," Carolina said. "The cottonwoods are out. The false cotton hangs in the air like snow."

Her mother looked at her with slight impatience. Carolina had the familiar sensation that she had managed to disappoint her without ever having been told the task.

"Your father says he met Turri by the lake today," her mother said.

Carolina nodded. "Sometimes he walks over."

"You know he is a married man."

Carolina nodded again.

Carolina's mother leaned forward. Her dress rustled like a pile of dry leaves. "You are not married yet," she said. "Until you are, you must be very careful."

The back of Carolina's neck tingled with shame at the implication. Heat rushed into her face. "There is nothing —" she began.

"That doesn't matter," her mother said. In the low light, her eyes were almost entirely consumed by the black of her pupils. "A girl does not have many choices. This is the most important one. There must be no whisper against your name until you are married."

Carolina stared at her like a fascinated animal. "After you are married," her mother continued, "many things may happen. You will not speak of them. Neither will your husband, if he is a gentleman." She looked out the dark window. "Do you understand?"

Carolina nodded.

Her mother nodded as well, not at Carolina, but as if agreeing with words spoken by some other, inaudible voice. She leaned back into the divan.

"Will you ask Stefi to bring me some warm milk when you go?" she asked.

"Of course," Carolina said, rising.

She paused in the door, but her mother had already thrown her arm over her eyes, as if protecting them from some unbearable light in the sky.

Carolina rose the next morning while it was still dark and slipped down the stairs more by the touch of the railing than by sight.

She had slept only in fits, and when she was tired her eyes acted like prisms, warping some things, duplicating others. Now they found the starlight on the dew so dazzling that the whole yard blurred. In the forest, the trees doubled and bent. She blinked, and they were straight again. She could still see some stars beyond the unreliable silhouettes of the topmost branches, but when she tried to focus on them, they flared into full suns or winked out altogether. Despite all this, she reached her house, sank down into the rumpled velvets on her couch, and gave herself up gratefully to a second sleep.

When she woke, afternoon sun streamed through the scarves in the windows, leaving the faintest traces of their design where the light landed. The ghost of a peacock bloomed in the dark folds of a blanket. A lily dissolved on her desk. Carolina pushed the covers away and lifted the corner of the simple blue scarf in the front window. Turri lay on his back on the bank, his eyes closed, his hands comforting each other on his chest. He looked just as familiar to her as the trees that shaded the opposite banks, and her heart greeted him with the same welcome. The world around him was clear again, each tree where it belonged, each reed as she remembered. Every bit of glowing cottonwood that floated over the black mirror of the lake was crisp and perfect.

She let the scarf fall back into place and went out to meet him.

For days afterward, Carolina imagined her father's footsteps on the grass, thought she heard him breaking twigs in the woods, or confused the bright flashes of bird wings glimpsed through the trees for a scrap of silk at his neck. But as the days turned to weeks, the weeks completed a season, and the leaves of late summer dropped so that she could see clearly through the trees, she realized that he wasn't coming to surprise her again. In fact, even the innocent visits he had been used to making on his haphazard rambles had stopped. It was a pattern she remembered, finally, from her childhood. Her father hated to punish her, so when he caught her in the act of some mischief, he went to great lengths not to catch her again. If he discovered her happily dunking sections of a mutilated lemon directly into the sugar jar, he issued a strict reprimand, but then he avoided the kitchen as if it had ceased to exist, sometimes for weeks on end. The fact that her misbehavior caused her father such obvious distress had always pained Carolina and made her want to do better. But now, when she felt he had misunderstood her so deeply, his absence simply came as a relief.

Just as the lake forgot the impact of a stone or the touch of the wind, Carolina and Turri returned to their familiar habits. That fall, he made an intricate set of wings out of saplings and twigs, copying from the skeleton of some small bird he unearthed during a walk through the forest. Carolina helped him line the frame with fallen leaves, which Turri half hoped might have similar properties to feathers. After weeks of work, Turri tested them himself with a jump from the roof of Carolina's house. He landed with a spectacular crash that seemed to come as no surprise to him at all. That night he returned with the now-useless contraption. As Carolina watched from the shore, he climbed back on the roof, set the damaged wings on fire, and launched them over the few paces of land between the house and the lake. The sudden burst of flame as air rushed over the burning frame gave the wings a strange, wobbly lift for one short moment. Then they swooped dangerously low, showering Carolina with red sparks before crashing into the lake with an enormous splash and hiss. Steam rose into the night, tinted orange by the surviving fire.

Some of the bones of the contraption still glowed fierce red as they sank through the dark water.

In mid-December a deep freeze set in, closing the last small patch of open water where the black ducks had swum melancholy circles as the rest of the lake was lost to them. When the cold hadn't broken after a week, Turri began to harvest ice from the edges of the lake just beyond the reeds, sawing out over a thousand brick-sized blocks to build a castle on the heart of the lake: four modest walls with a pair of turrets facing the small house on shore. The day before he completed it, the weather changed. The temperature climbed so high it felt like spring, and in the forest it rained all morning as ice melted from the grateful branches and dropped down into the thick mud below. The cloudy walls of the castle began to shine as the scuffs of Turri's saw melted away. All morning, he fought a losing battle with the sun, packing wet snow around the foundation and arranging and rearranging insufficient groups of tarps. But when the thick layer of ice that covered the whole lake began to creak and moan in the early afternoon, Carolina came out of her house and insisted that he come back to shore. Less than an hour later, the entire

54

structure crashed through into the frigid water, resurfacing as a jumble of jagged icebergs. When night fell, the bobbing chunks of ice froze into a spiky wound that marked the smooth surface for the rest of the winter.

Christmas Day, Carolina made her way to the lake through the new fall of powdery snow on the forest floor, clutching a box of marzipan and oranges. When she arrived at her house, she could see the unsteady light of a fire within already casting blue shadows on the snow outside. Turri was waiting with his overcoat still on, although he'd clearly been there for so long that the bright color that cold always called up in his face had faded away. On the table beside him stood a small elephant in blue enamel, about as tall as Carolina's thumb, its legs joined to its body at strange angles. A wheel like a captain might use to guide a ship protruded from the creature's right side.

Carolina set her box down on the desk and lifted the top to reveal the hand-painted pastries and oranges.

"Would you like a piece?" she said.

Turri shook his head. "I just lost a marzipan-eating contest with Antonio," he told her.

Carolina selected a bunch of sugar-coated

grapes for herself and closed the box.

"I don't know why elephants always seem so sad," she said, looking at the little figure.

"Wind it up," Turri said.

Carolina set the creature on her palm and lifted it to her face so that they could see eye to eye.

"The wheel," Turri said. "You turn it."

Carolina twisted the wheel. Slowly, the enameled feet began to move. First both right legs took a step, then both the left.

Turri broke into a proud grin. "Put it on the table," he said. "Watch it!"

Carolina set the toy down carefully on the desk. It marched gamely over an entire field of writing paper and came to a stop just before the marzipan box, regarding it with all the wonder and respect with which an explorer might confront a new mountain.

"I made it for you," Turri said with barely contained excitement.

"Thank you," Carolina said, gazing down at the gift.

Turri took her hand.

Surprised, Carolina looked at him.

"You know that I love you," he said.

The words rang in her mind like an alarm bell.

"I know," she said, and took her hand away.

■ ■ ■ ■

The following spring, when Carolina was seventeen, Pietro marked his twenty-fourth birthday, which meant that he stood just one year shy of the age of majority his father had stipulated in his will. But for Pietro to receive full control of his lands and property, his father had also dictated that he should be married. Pietro confronted this requirement with his customary goodwill. "I guess the old man knew what was best for me!" he said at party after party, shrugging with a mixture of mischief and ruefulness that made the girls shiver with hope and their parents nod in approval.

Carolina received this news with a terror so sweet she could barely distinguish it from thrill. It was impossible that he should choose her, but: he must choose somebody. Like a child with a lottery ticket, she understood the slimness of her chance, but until another name was called, while her paper ticket melted in her damp hand, she had just as much right to dream of stepping up to receive the prize as anyone. Her fantasies focused and became simple. She returned the pirates and invisible ink of her youthful dreams to the prop boxes in her mind, and began to construct realistic prayers: he might find her on the road during a cloud-burst and give her a ride home. He might catch her glance across a crowded room, and smile. These new dreams were so modest that they never lasted any longer than a moment. Carolina never knew what might happen after she smiled back, or he lifted her onto his mare.

Nobody, including Carolina and perhaps Pietro himself, ever knew why he began to single her out halfway through that season. Her mother was a remarkable beauty, which is what had led Carolina's father to pick her from the crowd of local girls on his two-week holiday to a seaside town so many years ago. Carolina, though slightly taller than her mother, had inherited her thick dark hair, small waist, and pale, perfect face. But her eyes were her father's, dark under a strong brow, rather than her mother's delicate blue. The effect was so compelling that it struck many boys speechless and made the rest want to torment her in revenge, a project they embarked on so early in her memory that she never even thought to resent their taunts, but simply navigated them as she would any feature of her small landscape: a river to be crossed, or a hole to step around.

But her beauty alone was not sufficient to explain Pietro's interest. There were other beautiful girls who were not nearly as strange or difficult. They had gold hair as smooth as coiled wheat, rounder figures, pale hands that had not grown chapped from plucking at things in the forest. And that spring, every charm was on display, every gem and flower arranged to capture Pietro's heart. Carolina could hardly have won it by outshining them.

In fact, it might have been her terror that originally caught his attention.

In early June, after a blur of spring parties during which nobody, including those who considered themselves his closest friends, was able to penetrate the mystery of Pietro's intentions, Carolina turned her head as she walked up the stairs to the Ricci ballroom and found Pietro on the step beside her. When she had seen him last, he was halfway across the great hall below, where the servants had constructed a fragile canopy of twine from which a thousand votive candles dangled in colored glasses just above the heads of the guests. Carolina wasn't actually hoping to dance: during all of the dozen parties since the season opened, Pietro hadn't asked her once, and with the fierce, foolish loyalty of first love, she had turned away all other requests. Her plan was to stop on the landing and look down through the lights as everyone else looked up at them, something like the way God must peer down at the earth through the stars.

But before she reached the landing, Pietro had bounded up the stairs behind her, two at a time. He wasn't coming after her — he made that clear enough by leaping another two steps past her before he halted midstride, perhaps distracted from his goal by her pretty face.

"Carolina!" he said.

Carolina was always somewhat bewildered when confronted with Pietro in the flesh, who spoke and acted so differently than the Pietro of her daydreams. In this emergency, she could only stare back at him, thrilled but speechless.

Pietro raised his eyebrows. "They are playing a *monferrina* later," he said. "You will save it for me?" He grinned, certain that he was offering a gift that would please them both.

Fear froze Carolina's hands to fists in the folds of her dress. The *monferrina* was a complicated courting dance, new to their valley that year, and she still didn't know it. There was no way she could dance one as

Pietro's partner, with all eyes on her. She looked down at the blue carpet, then glanced over the marble balustrade at the canopy of flames in their colored glass. "No, thank you," she said.

Pietro's grin widened. This was a tactic he was familiar with, and easily enough disposed of. He laid a hand on his chest, mocking real agony. "But you will break my heart!" he said.

His refusal to let her go with grace woke anger in Carolina, warm enough to melt the fear that froze her fingers. She gathered her skirts and climbed the next step. "I don't think so," she said, and swept past him.

At the top of the stairs, she hesitated. She had arrived at a long balcony that overlooked the grand staircase and the hall below. Directly in front of her, several sets of doors opened into the ballroom. To her right, at the far end of the balcony, was a window at least three times her height, turned mirror by the night. At the other end of the balcony, to her left, was a door. She hurried toward it, passing through the few guests scattered along the way without a glance or a greeting. The knob turned easily under her hand. The room inside was completely dark, except for faint traces of

61

stars distorted by towering windows.

Turri laughed.

His shape pulled itself free from the mass of shadows below the nearest window. A dark volume waved in his hand.

"I'm reading about steam engines by moonlight," he said. "I can only make out about half of it, so it's become a kind of experiment. Everything I can't see, I have to invent."

Comforted by his voice, Carolina took a few steps into the darkness.

"Be careful," he said. "I banged my shins on half a dozen end tables on my way over here."

She paused in the dark and reached out. Her hands described the diameter of an awkward half circle but found nothing.

"Actually, there are only two tables," Turri amended. "And then a statue of a girl, presented among the other furniture on a low stand instead of a pedestal, so that an unsuspecting man might find himself suddenly face-to-face with her."

As Carolina's eyes adjusted to the low light, tall shelves began to emerge between the windows. She could pick out the shapes of two tables nearby, but no white stone glimmered in the gloom.

"Really?" she said.

"You don't see her?" he asked.

A knock sounded on the door.

Carefully, Carolina turned in the dark. The knock sounded again.

She pulled the door open. A narrow triangle of yellow light split the room. Pietro stood outside, his hands clasped behind him like an unhappy child. "Carolina!" he exclaimed, with all the emotion of a shipwrecked sailor who could scarcely believe that his rescuers had arrived. Then he paused, trying to read her face. After a moment, he gave up and plunged on.

"They have sent some of the musicians to the garden with lanterns," he said. "Would you care to join me there?"

Behind Carolina, a book closed in the darkness. Carolina glanced back, but Turri remained silent, his shadow dissolved among the rest.

Pietro shuffled uncertainly, all his brashness forgotten.

For the first time, she pitied him.

"Thank you," she said, and took his arm.

Their conversation that evening was of no consequence. Pietro misidentified several constellations and praised the quality of the wine, speaking with unnatural stiffness, as if struggling to remember a lesson a tutor had tried to teach him years ago, when he hadn't seen any reason yet to learn it. Carolina began to breathe almost naturally after the first several quartets. By the end of the evening, she had confided to him that she wasn't convinced that there really *were* constellations: every time she looked at the sky, it seemed to have changed slightly from the last time, although she could never pick out exactly which of the thousands of lights had shifted, to prove her point. "Everyone says the stars are fixed," she told him. "But no one ever says what holds them there."

"But how could we know that?" Pietro asked somewhat plaintively.

As the evening wore on, they were interrupted several times by the greetings of his friends, as well as a steady stream of young ladies who approached their garden bench and spoke to Pietro as if he were the only one sitting there. But Pietro didn't leave Carolina's side. Finally the faint clatter of departing carriages began to drift over the garden wall. The musicians played their final piece, collected their instruments, and departed after a minor scuffle when the cello ran aground in the dark on a bed of lilies.

"Carolina," Pietro said. His tone was urgent, the prelude to a confession or an announcement. But when she turned to him, he seemed to be looking to her for some answer. Confused, she dropped her gaze.

"It's so late," she said. "They'll think we've been captured by gypsies."

This was a joke, but Pietro shook his head earnestly. "They could never take you from me," he promised.

He rose and offered her his arm. Carolina stood to take it, then let him lead her across the garden to the house, concentrating with all her might on the difficult task of walking and breathing at the same time.

The following week, Pietro managed to coax Carolina onto the dance floor for a string of more familiar dances, and the other girls ceased to greet her in the halls, as if she had turned invisible. A few days later, Pietro sent a servant to Carolina's home with an enormous bundle of roses that the old man asserted Pietro had cut from the garden himself, a claim borne out by the fact that the massive jumble of thorns included what seemed to be several entire rosebushes, lopped off just above the root. Pietro would be honored, the old man added, if Carolina would allow him the pleasure of paying her a visit.

This was unprecedented.

From time to time, Pietro had seemed to have favorites among the local girls, picking one as his partner for a long string of dances, or even seeking a particular young lady out over the course of several events before he lost interest. He was able to do this with impunity because he never embarrassed the girls or their families by taking even the smallest steps into the realm of formal courtship: afternoon visits or family dinners. Carolina was the first girl in the valley to receive this attention.

Her father, a sporadic but deeply sentimental gardener, was shocked by the brutalization of Pietro's rosebushes and unimpressed with his request to see Carolina.

"I feel like I ought to send these outside and have them planted again," he said, glowering down at the heap of branches and blossoms that trembled on their hall table.

"No, no!" Carolina gasped. She thrust her hands among the red-green leaves, choked off a cry as thorns dug into her palms and fingers, and drew them back.

At the open door, the old man waited in the strong noon light.

"Tomorrow?" Carolina asked, pleading.

Her father shook his head at the tangle of roses. Then he nodded.

With the racing heart and finely tuned bravado of a young queen addressing her subjects for the first time, Carolina turned to the old man. "He may come tomorrow," she told him.

Lemon trees were Carolina's father's inheritance, but his love for them was real: as a boy, he had insisted that the gardener plant half a dozen lemon saplings in the family garden so that when he was a man he would not have to walk all the way down to the groves to pick a flower or a piece of fruit. These young trees now shaded the whole Fantoni garden. Their gardener constantly complained that he was the only man in the valley asked to coax flowers from their beds each year without the help of sunlight, to which Carolina's father invariably replied that great obstacles were the tutors of great men.

The day of Pietro's first visit, spring's blossoms had fallen from the lemon tree branches, but their leaves still glowed like new growth, not yet touched by the heat that would darken them to evergreen. Carolina sat beneath them breathless but perfectly still, ready to believe anything. If it was true, as his note claimed, that Pietro would arrive at any moment to pass an hour with her in the garden, then any number of her other most outlandish fantasies were possible as well. The sky might suddenly roll up as the priest sometimes threatened, revealing the other world that men could only glimpse now in shadows and mirages, a world Carolina had suspected the existence of long before her haphazard introduction to theology because of an intermittent but deeply felt sense that even the most solid things lacked real weight, and that, if she only knew the trick, it would be a simple thing to see through them.

The shadows on the new grass wavered, but didn't give way.

"Carolina?" Pietro's voice was as unfamiliar as a stranger's.

Carolina froze like a creature startled in the forest. Before her reason really returned, Pietro had spotted her through the trees. He strode toward her, grinning.

"Your mother said I would find you here," he called, pushing through the young branches. Then he stood over her, so handsome that she simply stared back up at him, all her thoughts vanquished.

"She says she can't keep you in the house, summer or winter," Pietro teased.

"I like the lake and the garden," Carolina told him, listening to herself speak with the same curiosity with which she might eavesdrop on a couple whispering beside her at a dance, and with the same lack of certainty about what she might say next.

Pietro sat down beside her on the bench. He studied her face carefully for a moment. Then he took her hand. The warmth of it surprised her, as it had the first time they danced, when she had also been surprised to realize that, like other men, he needed to breathe. He smiled. "I thought of you all night," he told her. "I didn't fall asleep until dawn, and when I woke up I came straight here."

"Sometimes I can't sleep," Carolina agreed.

"But I can always sleep," Pietro said eagerly, and proceeded to tell her the story of a raucous brawl during which his friends had turned a chair to kindling and shattered two windows and one of their noses while he slept like a child on a couch in the center of the melee. When she smiled at this, he launched into another, apparently following the theme of brawls, in which a friend of his had taken a wild shot at another and accidentally killed a horse outside in the street, a fact that they discovered only hours later, when they stepped outside to find the poor beast lying dead in the rain.

Over the next week, he told her any number of stories and secrets. The stories he always told as if he were speaking to a small crowd, even when Carolina was the only one there: his voice a little too loud, his gestures a little too broad, glancing away from her face from time to time as if trying to catch another pair of eyes. Some of these stories she knew already, since they had long since passed into local legend: the Rossi fire, the marzipan feasts, the night he had hung Ricardo Bianchi, hog-tied, from the cleft of a fig tree.

The story of his outlandish grief over his mother's death was also well traveled in the valley: instead of throwing the handful of petals onto his mother's casket as he had been instructed, the five-year-old Pietro had leapt into the grave with her, and when Pietro refused to take the many hands that were held out to pull him back up, a groom had been forced to climb down and retrieve him. Every step the boy or the man had taken in the course of the struggle had resounded with a horrible echo on the wooden box, a sound nobody in attendance had yet forgotten. But now Pietro confessed to Carolina that his grief hadn't left him in the floods of angry tears he cried in the weeks after his mother's death: it had been his constant childhood companion. In fact, his gardener still kept his trowels and shovels under lock and key out of habit from Pietro's boyhood, when, at any chance, Pietro would sneak into the gardener's shed to steal the tools and mount another assault on the earth that covered his mother's grave.

"I never told another girl this," he told her, looking into her eyes with surprise and a certain curious expectation, as if waiting for her to explain to him why he had chosen her.

But it was a mystery to Carolina as well. She had never asked for his secrets, and she wasn't sure she wanted them. They seemed like confessions to her, not the pretty trinkets she had thought a new lover would confide. She felt their weight, and her own inability to heal or absolve, and it frightened her. She found herself wishing for the Pietro her heart had constructed over the previous years: sure-footed, understanding, and fearless, to come rescue her from Pietro himself as he rambled on at her side. The wish made her dizzy.

Still, Pietro didn't seem to tire of their conversations, or of her. At her mother's invitation, he returned for dinner the night after his first visit, and from then the pattern was set. Each day, he arrived at Carolina's home on some pretext: bearing a brace of bloodied rabbits he had killed that morning because her father admitted to a fondness for them; carrying a bottle of his father's best wine, which he hoped might alleviate the headache her mother had complained of the previous day; or insisting, to her father's delight, that the shade of her garden was simply much more pleasant than the bright sunlight in his, so that he couldn't help but prefer to spend his time in it.

Carolina lived through those first days with Pietro half believing that it was all a dream from which she might awake at any moment, and she moved through her days as if even the slightest sound or movement might cause the whole world to dissolve. It was the end of the week before she remembered that she had not seen her lake for days, a realization that came to her as she watched a hard summer rain beat down on her father's drive, cutting slender streams through the gravel. It was Sunday. The night before, at the Rosetti gala, Pietro had danced over half the dances with her and spent most of the rest at her side under one of the enormous goose-feather fans Silvia Rosetti had ordered affixed to her ballroom walls, large enough that, in an emergency, they might also serve as wings for a grown man. During one of the more sentimental waltzes, Pietro had nodded at a dancer in a military jacket and repeated a story that he had told her only days before: "When I was a young man," he murmured, with all the urgency of a new secret, "my only dream was to die in battle. I never thought I would live to be this old."

Carolina had felt the gaze of a pair of girls on the other side of the room. When her eyes met theirs, they quickly turned away. She looked back at Pietro, struggling to compose her face into an expression of surprise and sympathy. "I am so glad you were wrong," she said, as she had the first time he had told her.

With great emotion, he had taken her hand in both of his.

No word had come yet from him today. The little storm soon blew itself out. When the slim rivers in the driveway had grown still, reflecting the white sky, Carolina rose and went out.

Turri stood at the water's edge, soaking wet, his thin shirt sticking to his skin in large patches.

"You could have gone inside," Carolina called.

Turri glanced back at her and grinned.

"Have you been swimming?" she asked when she reached him.

He shook his head. "I was studying the rain."

"What did you learn?" she asked.

The sun was still hidden by a thin haze that covered the whole visible sky, but even from there it burned bright enough to make the water on his temples shine.

"I was sleeping on the bank," he said. "I woke up when it started to rain. I sat up to go to the house, but then I thought, I wonder what I'll see if I just lie here and look up?"

"What did you see?" she asked.

"Rain," he said, grinning again. "And then it gets in your eyes, and you can't see anything."

Turri didn't ask about her absence, and she didn't mention Pietro to him, although it was impossible that he hadn't heard the rumors. Instead, they flipped her rowboat upright and pushed out onto the lake together, Carolina at the oars and Turri sprawled in the bow. His damp clothes dried as the sunlight burned off the remaining clouds. Carolina let the oars drift, hypnotized by the thousand ways the forest changed each time the boat swung a breath to the right or a breath to the left. Finally the sun broke free from the clouds completely. As she raised her hand to shield her eyes, she realized she had no sense of how much time had passed. Suddenly wide awake with worry, she rowed the few strokes back to land and then, at Turri's request, pushed him back out onto the water again.

When she returned to the house, a servant told her that Pietro had already arrived, and that her mother had taken him to the greenhouse. Her father had built the glass structure on the back lawn when Carolina was seven, again over the objections of his exasperated gardener, so that her mother could always have the southern blossoms she remembered from her youth. Today, the glass panels were still fogged from the rain.

"Carolina!" Pietro exclaimed, as if she were a ship returning from an indefinite journey.

"Where have you been?" her mother asked, a note of warning in her voice.

Carolina paused in the door of the humid room. On their damp wooden tables, lilies, freesia, and a gang of waxy orchids waited for her answer. "I went to the lake," she said. "Turri has been investigating the rain."

"Turri?" Pietro said broadly, as if helping

a friend to set up the punch line of a well-known joke.

"They have been friends since she was a child," Carolina's mother added quickly.

"So have I!" Pietro said, soldiering through the joke himself since nobody else had chimed in. "He filled the river with soap bubbles when we were boys. All the reeds were choked with foam. I saw a red finch fly off with a bit hanging from his beak, just like an old man with a beard."

He paused, listening for laughter, and seemed surprised, as he so often did, to find that the crowd he had been speaking to had dwindled again to just the two women who had been in the room with him when he began. When neither Carolina nor her mother spoke, his face clouded. Then an explanation seemed to come to him. He strode quickly through the plants, took Carolina's hand, and kissed it. "When will you take me to your lake?" he asked.

Because she could not imagine this, Carolina did not answer.

After a moment, Pietro smiled indulgently. "That's all right," he said. "It is better if sweethearts keep some secrets."

The following weekend, as a small choir of violins wavered in unison about some great disappointment in their distant past, Pietro kissed her for the first time. They stood in the shelter of a grotto below the verandah of the Conti house. Above them, all their neighbors spun in circles under torches that burned at the borders of the makeshift dance floor.

His kiss was gentle, but urgent. When he released her, she dropped her head onto his chest, her face hot and her breath fast. No one had ever kissed her before, and nothing she had heard or seen had prepared her for the insistent warmth that spread through her limbs.

He laughed, stroking her thick hair.

Carolina held fistfuls of his jacket in both hands, waiting for the heat to pass. Instead, it grew stronger, singing louder than the violins.

She lifted her face. "Again," she said.

A month later, as August's last blossoms began to fade, Pietro dropped to one knee as her father watched from his post by the fireplace's empty grate and her mother half rose from the couch where she lay. He extracted a small piece of crumpled paper from his pocket and unwrapped it to reveal his mother's diamond ring, which glittered like a piece of ice melted down to almost nothing by the morning sun.

Refusing him was impossible.

Carolina was never sure when the blindness had first set in. Looking back through the dim and crowded closets of her mind, she found half a dozen days, spread over a decade: the time when, as a child, she had rubbed her eyes so hard that the world had been dappled for hours with red and green shadows; the way that everyone else seemed to get used to the dark long before her eyes could pick shapes out; a day when she hit her head falling out of a tree and woke to find the whole world unmoored, turning as gently as a leaf might turn on the surface of her lake. Every trick her eyes had ever played came back to her: birds that proved to be only flowers blooming on a branch; flowers that suddenly awoke, spread their wings, and proved themselves birds.

But it was the autumn after Pietro's proposal, when she was eighteen years old, that the blindness became undeniable. Later she realized that it must have begun at the borders of her vision and worked its way in like twilight: so slowly that no change was noticeable from one moment to the next, but so steadily that by the time she recognized evening setting in, true night seemed to be only a breath away. As the trees released their leaves, she grew uneasy. She could hear the ringing splash of a loon landing on the lake, but the corner of her eye wouldn't catch its motion. Squirrels teased her from the trees, but by the time she turned her head to see them, they had vanished.

When that season's last leaves sank to the bottom of the lake, leaving the forest bare, Carolina gazed across the black water at the line of seven trees that her father had allowed to stand when he first cleared the land: a generous old willow, a wild apple, a junk tree with smooth gray bark, an oak, a sapling and a pair of slim birch rooted like twins or lovers, so close that their branches rattled together in the wind. Counting them all had been a favorite game when she was a child, and was still a comfort as she grew. But now her vision could not take them all in. She could see the willow, or the twins: never both in the same glance. For the first time, she understood that she was going blind.

The realization came to her with all the force of a conversion. Like a new believer, she could never see the world the same way again, whether she kept her faith or lost it. But the shape of the new world, the tempo of its liturgy, the properties of its angels and demons, was still a mystery.

For most of the winter, Carolina tested her blindness. For instance: how fast did it move? Perhaps, having taken all her life to reach this point, it might take another twenty years to claim another fraction of her sight. With scientific precision that would have made Turri proud, she sketched the trees on the opposite bank and marked off what she could see when she faced them dead on from the top step of her house. In November she could take in five trees, bounded by the willow and the sapling. By the New Year, the sapling had vanished. When darkness began to swallow up the willow as well, she tried to tell her mother and father. When the willow was extinguished, she told Pietro.

By this time, Pietro had learned enough about her habits to recognize that she was not like the other young ladies of his acquaintance, and had taken to calling her "my stranger." Her announcement seemed to him to be just another piece of happy nonsense, like her affection for her poorly conceived lake with its muddy banks, or her inexplicable patience with Turri's experiments.

Her parents had long since forgotten her attempts to warn them. Her father was engaged in a war of attrition with the gardener, who insisted that, if he were to cut all the flowers her father demanded for Carolina's wedding, the garden itself, where the reception was to be held, would have all the charm of a desert — to which her father replied that all men of genius are mocked by their own servants. Carolina's mother still left her room infrequently, but a steady stream of servants and delivery boys now came and went, bearing fruit, chocolates, china, silver, silks, brocade and lace, and a parade of gifts sent ahead by the hundreds of invited guests.

Carolina always opened these gifts in her mother's company, so as her sight was leaving her she handled some of the most beautiful things she had ever seen: an enameled box, robin's egg blue, wavy like watered silk, lined in rose velvet; a spiral shell the size of her fist, with a silver lid, for holding salt; sheets embroidered with lemon blossoms and vines; a glass candy dish the color of blood; a serving tray of silver beaten into the shape of a giant grape leaf, with a life-size bunch of cold silver grapes clustered under the curve of the handle and a small bird perched on the opposite rim, gazing at the metal fruit with longing.

At first, Carolina tried to memorize these

things. She began a careful catalog in her mind, closed her eyes, and quizzed herself. But she quickly discovered that each time she called up an object in her memory, it eroded or changed. The bird on the tray, which had seemed so hopeful at her first glance, grew melancholy in her mind and developed jeweled eyes: now onyx, now sapphire, so that each time she looked at the actual tray again she had the sense that it was not quite as beautiful as it had been. The enameled box opened in her unreliable memory to reveal white and brown speckled eggs, pale gray stones worn smooth by the river, loose diamonds. Eventually she gave up the project of memorization, but she continued to try to soak up as much of the world as she could take in: the candlelight in her mother's room, waterbirds landing on her lake, the folds of her white dress as the seamstress fitted it, added a hundred yards of lace, and fitted it again. The world had trouble withstanding her searching gaze. The blindness at the corners of her vision and the black water of her lake melded into a thick shadow that threatened to swallow up the sky and trees she could still see. The forest seemed to lose its depth and flatten, as if it were only painted on a scrim hung by some traveling theater company.

Everything gave the impression that it was in danger of giving way to reveal whatever horror or wonder the seen world now obscured.

But the blindness never relented. The week before her wedding she lost the oak, leaving only the junk tree and the wild apple, which overnight had burst into full bloom, like a breathless bride adorned in white, trembling with joy over the slightest breeze.

This was when she had told Turri.

The spring that Carolina was born, her mother had planted rows and rows of white rosebushes in anticipation of her daughter's wedding day. Today, their branches graced the arch of the church door, held in place with swags of cheesecloth, varied here and there by the clouds of white blossoms Carolina's maid called starlight, or by long tufts of river grass. Roses littered the tables the servants had arranged the evening before on the lawn, where two kitchen maids now stood guard against further attempts by a strapping black crow who had neatly stolen a pair of forks and a shining knife in the small hours of the morning, before a stable boy, defending his own honor in the matter, discovered the true thief and surprised the bird into dropping the spoon that would have completed his setting. Roses lay in heaps on Carolina's dressing table as her maid helped her into her dress and her mother toyed with her hair. The blindness had advanced so far that she saw the world now as if peering through a sheet of rolled paper — a few sentences on a page, a single face. It made the whole thought of marrying Pietro, which had always seemed to her like a strange dream she might wake from at any moment, seem even more unreal.

At the church, her failing eyes reduced the blossoms that wound over the church door to a haze of white and green, and her gathered neighbors and relatives to a murmuring mist. She made her way down the aisle by memory and guesswork, taking small steps to avoid stumbling over her yards of silk and lace, catching her balance from time to time when she trod on one of the unfortunate roses that had been scattered in her honor on the worn stones. About halfway down, she caught the sound of a familiar voice and turned to see Turri. He gazed back at her as if it were any other day, and he was only waiting for an answer or her next move in a game. Beside him, Sophia stared up at her with the unreasoned but unerring cunning of a cat, taking in every detail of her dress with greed and suspicion.

Then Carolina looked back at the altar where a hundred candles wavered, pale in the strong afternoon light, dropping hot wax onto the faces of the uncomplaining crowd of asters and blue phlox massed at their feet. Pietro stood beside the priest, the light bending all around him: handsome, certain, grinning.

"You're like a bird," Pietro complained. "Hold still. The ocean can't run away."

Carolina, who had been turning her head swiftly from side to side in the vain hope of capturing the entire shoreline in a single glance, did as he said. The vast expanse of white sand and the blue band of ocean that stretched beyond it to the sky vanished, replaced by the sea in cameo, a glimmering oval fragment small enough to dangle from a woman's neck, surrounded by darkness.

Pietro turned her face to his and kissed it.

"You are so beautiful," he whispered. "Maybe I will never love you more than this."

Darkness had never frightened Carolina, but during the blazing seaside days of her honeymoon, it became a friend. The bright ocean was a real torment to her, with all the light from a thousand waves streaming into her limited eyes, but when night came, she was again equal: the whole world had also gone blind. In fact, she had the advantage. The blindness had cured her of superstition about the secret qualities of darkness, the dread that things shifted and became strange when not governed by a human eye. Through long association, she had learned that the darkness had no power to alter what it hid. Her hairbrush or pen might be obscured by the blindness, but when she reached for them, they were the same as they had always been. As a result, shadows no longer held any magic for her. Her confidence remained even as the evening sky sank from blue to black. By night, she was even more sure-footed than Pietro, whose dependence on the sunlight made him clumsy in the dark. So she was the one who led him through the unlit corners of the seaside town after the shops had closed and the restaurants had emptied out, as the waiters poured buckets of water onto the stones to wash away the evidence of that evening's feasts, and gypsy music began to drift through certain open windows.

Pietro loved these rambles, willing to bear with his young wife's caprices for the opportunity they offered him to catch at the dim curves of her retreating figure in a close alley, or press her against the walls of some back street. He was an ardent but gentle lover, most tender with her when freed from the impossible task of forcing his deepest feelings to the surface as words. Carolina was half thrilled and half terrified by the way he changed in the dark: shocked by the places his hands sought out and by the way her own body rose and burned under them, amazed to find that her own touch could make him flinch or groan, but most of all grateful for a world in which only taste and touch, sound and smell, mattered, where, even if she did open her eyes, the horizon had shrunk to just what she could still take in: Pietro's eyes, the back of his neck, her finger caught in his teeth.

Each day, however, was a new mystery. Rising from their shared bed, they dressed quickly, like the first man and woman, newly naked and ashamed. Their meals were passed in long silences, punctuated by half-remembered pleasantries. At a loss, Pietro returned again and again to the theme of her beauty, which he earnestly believed must please her as much as it pleased him.

"I think the angels were God's practice," he would say, reaching out to catch a handful of her hair. "To make this pretty head."

Carolina could not think of what to say to this. The angels of her catechism were fearsome men and she was terrified to speak of God, in case he might remember her and speed the curse he had chosen. Furthermore, Pietro didn't seem to want his compliments returned. In the first days of the honeymoon, confused by the praise, she had retreated into basic etiquette.

"Your eyes are beautiful as well," she said.

For an instant, he had smiled like a petted child, but just as quickly the light of pride was lost in a frown. "Beauty is a blind guide in a man," he told her, probably in the same stern tones it had been told to him.

"I'm sorry," she ventured.

"There is no need," he said, more gently.

Carolina couldn't remember this restraint in the months of their courtship, but the moments they had spent alone together before their marriage amounted to mere hours, spent in breathless snatches behind hedges and in hallways, exchanging burning kisses, groping blindly for whatever might be hidden beneath the lace at her breast or in the hollow of his hand. Beyond that, under the watchful eye of her family, they had only flirted and teased until the day, as her mother wept quietly, Carolina had raised him from his knees.

"Would you like to go dancing tonight?" Pietro asked one evening, joining Carolina on the balcony. "They are building a pavilion on the beach."

The lengths of white gauze that shut out the morning light twisted around them like the tethered ghosts of ocean breezes. The sun had just vanished into the horizon and in the gloaming below lights had begun to appear, marking the path of the streets, the entrances of restaurants, the stands where night vendors peddled wine and fruit to lovers and young families at the water's edge.

When she didn't answer immediately, he nuzzled her neck like a favored horse.

"We don't have to dance," he said. "You give me a command."

Carolina turned in the circle of his arms and looked up at him. Surrounded by darkness, his handsome face was as frank and hopeful as a child's.

In despair, she closed her eyes.

Pietro kissed them.

Her husband's property bounded her father's. In fact, the river that fed her lake flowed into it from Pietro's land. A bend in the water was visible from Pietro's house, at the foot of a gentle slope that rolled down to a landing area where a pair of old boats dozed in the sun.

On the first morning after their return from the ocean, Carolina awoke to find herself alone. Pietro's sheets were thrown back, already cold. Slightly giddy with the sudden freedom from his constant company, she dressed and found her way down the front stairs and out the door, moving toward her lake with the compulsion of a migrating bird that follows a map buried deeper in his mind than his own thoughts. She spent the day staring at the black water. Her sight had dwindled now so that her field of vision was almost completely overtaken by shadow, with two small bright spots through which she could still see the world, as if through windows on the other side of a room. Through them, she watched the mist burn away and the white sky appear in reflection on the lake. Mirrored clouds drifted across the surface and vanished in the weeds. Waterbirds landed with a rush of back-beating wings and threw the whole world into chaos.

As evening fell, she thrashed back through the waist-high grass that grew along the river, to Pietro's house.

She found him in the kitchen, eating a cold chicken.

"Where have you been hiding?" he asked.

"Where do you think?" she said.

This wasn't a joke, but on another day he might have taken it for one and smiled. When he didn't, Carolina crossed to where he sat, leaned over him, and pressed her face against his. He smelled as if he had just come in from riding — traces of new sweat and the sweet, dusty smell of feed from the barn.

"Where have you been?" she asked.

Pietro planted a greasy kiss on her cheek. "I bet you were out there all day dreaming without anything to eat," he said. He lifted a piece of chicken from the cloth on the table. "Well? Aren't you hungry?"

Because there was no path from her new home to her lake, Carolina went by a different route each day: through the pines that faced Pietro's house just beyond the great lawn, or tramping down waist-high swamp grass along the river. In her new rooms, the trunks and boxes of her things, carefully packed by her mother's maids, stood untouched by her until, in exasperation, a pair of Pietro's servants broke them open, hung her dresses in the wardrobes, and set her combs and vases on the vanity and tables, executing all these tasks with flawless precision to underscore their disapproval of Carolina's lack of interest in both her own things and her new home.

Three days after her return, Turri had still failed to appear.

The following morning, Carolina opened her window to watch the children of the servants in the side yard. Each figure flared up from the shadows of her blindness only when she looked directly down on them, almost as though she were spying through a glass. A pair of small girls gleefully flung feed at a crowd of white geese, as if their aim was to blind rather than feed the birds, who remained imperturbably greedy despite the hail of hard corn. Boys carried buckets of water from the well to the kitchen, shouting jokes and threats at the older girls, who went right on pinning up the morning linens as though they were deaf. The only exception was a tall girl of perhaps thirteen or fourteen who gave one boy an answer sharp enough that it seemed to freeze him in place for a long moment before he frowned in confusion and ran away. The girl's features were delicate, framed by a long fall of glossy black hair. She might have passed for an artist's angel at a distance, but the anger in her eyes was unmistakably of this world.

When one of the maids arrived with her

morning pitcher of water, Carolina tapped on the glass. "Who is that?" she asked, pointing to the girl.

"Liza," the maid said.

"Send her to me, please," Carolina said.

A few minutes later, the girl stood in Carolina's room, taking in all the rich details with furtive, eager glances she seemed to believe she took too quickly for Carolina to notice.

"Do you know where the Turri house is?" Carolina asked.

"It is the house on the hill, with the lions," the girl answered.

"Good," Carolina said, and pressed a letter into the girl's hand.

That afternoon, Carolina cut through the heart of the pine forest. The sunlight that filtered down through the needles melded into a bright halo at the limits of her vision, giving the trees and lake the aspect of a sacred painting.

Turri had arrived before her. He stood on the bank near her house and watched her make her way along the far side of the lake. As she approached, her vision split his face in two and interposed flashes of black water. Uneasy under his searching gaze, frustrated by her own sight, she went up to the house without a greeting. He followed.

"It is the same?" he asked, before she was even seated.

Hearing him speak the truth aloud, after keeping it in silence for so long, Carolina was seized with a sudden urge to deny everything and retreat with her parents and Pietro to the refuge of delusion for as long as it would shelter them. But the sound of Turri's voice also seemed to shake something loose: cut a weight free from her shoulders, throw a window open in the room.

She nodded and sank down on the couch. "The same," she said. "Maybe a little worse. It's hard to measure. It's worse with bright light. At night it's better."

"It will be easier for you if you stay away from bright light," Turri said, and turned the chair backward to straddle it. He must have come straight there on receiving her message: he still wore the scarred leather pants and loose workman's shirt he dressed in for the laboratory.

"It won't move as fast?" she asked quickly. "Can I stop it?"

Turri shook his head. "It will just be easier," he said.

While she was gone, some summer storm had torn apart one of her window scarves.

A large brown moth struggled through the remaining pink and violet threads. Gaining the narrow sill, it steadied itself, then began to walk the length of unvarnished wood, bearing its beautiful wings like an unfamiliar burden. When Carolina turned her head to see him, Turri was also gazing up at the insect.

"And you," Carolina asked, half from habit and half as a dash back to the safety of familiar shadows, "what have you been doing these past weeks?"

"I am building Sophia a new machine," he said.

"What does it do?"

"It boils an egg," he said. "She only needs to light a candle, and it will heat the water, deposit the egg for the required time, and lift it out again."

"But how does it know the time?" Carolina asked.

"I spent the week after your wedding crafting candles that burn an identical length each minute."

Carolina laughed. "Why don't you just give her a watch?" she asked. "Couldn't she keep the time herself?"

"She could," Turri said. "But she doesn't like eggs."

Perhaps frightened by Carolina's laughter,

the moth chose this moment to dive from its ledge, over Carolina's head. She buried her face in the pillows. When she raised it again, the moth had settled on the scarf in the opposite window, pressed flat, revealing wide, pale blue eyes on each wing.

"We can't kill it," Carolina said.

"No," Turri agreed, rising.

"You'll have to carry it out."

"I know." Deftly, Turri unfastened the pins that held the scarf in place and caught the moth in the folds of fabric. Through the thin cloth, Carolina could see its great wings quiver. At the door, Turri let the scarf fall. The moth hesitated for a moment on his palm, then gathered its courage and lurched away.

"How long do I have?" Carolina asked.

Turri turned back to her like a shadow, his clothing and features erased by the bright light that streamed past him from the surface of her lake.

"You said it was like looking through rolled paper," he said, taking his seat again.

She nodded.

"Like opera glasses?" he asked. "Or even less, like a spy glass?"

"Like opera glasses," she said. "But as if someone is always folding them too close together, so you can't quite see through."

Turri frowned and looked down at the thick rug beside her bed.

"Turri," she said.

She could no longer see clearly enough to know whether the tears she thought she glimpsed in his blue eyes were real.

"Around the New Year," he said. "At the latest."

Several days later, Liza struggled out onto the verandah, where Carolina was reclining inside a fortress of screens she had erected against the light with the hope that she might still feel the afternoon breeze. The girl's thin arms were weighed down with half a dozen large leather-bound volumes. Pietro trailed behind her.

"They're from Turri!" he announced. "It's not winter yet! What does he think we want with books?"

Liza set her load carefully beside Carolina's couch and straightened. "Shall I bring the rest?" she asked.

"Of course!" Pietro said, waving impatiently. "Go ahead!"

Carolina reached for the first volume, then sat up and opened it at random. An extraordinary butterfly, fully five times life size, spread across the page, hand-tinted blue and black with flecks of gilt flaking from the tips of its wings.

"A moth!" Pietro said. "I'll be damned."

Carolina turned the page. A pair of butterflies balanced on a branch. A chrysalis hung below them. Inside the translucent casing, she could make out the large eyes and cramped legs of the altered insect, its wings folded like lengths of brocade on its back. The adults above it were faint blue, paler than the sky, their lacy wing tips fading to a rich cream, broken here and there by irregular bits of black, as if their maker had flicked a paintbrush after them as they escaped.

With an air of capitulation, Pietro sank down beside her and lifted the next volume. "Birds," he said. The next: "Chinese dress."

Carolina picked up another. "These are drawings of America," she said.

Liza soldiered out of the house with another seven volumes and laid them at Carolina's feet with enormous delicacy and suspicion, as if the books were both highly fragile and packed with explosives.

"Liza," Carolina said as the girl withdrew.

Liza turned, her hands deep in the pockets of her gray dress.

"Thank you," Carolina said. "Ask for a chocolate in the kitchen."

Without answer or thanks, Liza turned

away again.

"These are maps," Pietro said. "But they are too old to be accurate." He laughed. "Look at this!" His strong fingers pointed to a school of bare-breasted mermaids frolicking in a green sea, blissfully unaware of their proximity to the precipice of a great waterfall labeled *Finisterra.*

Pietro threw his arm around her and kissed her cheek, her mouth, her neck. Then he stood up, shaking his head. "Turri is a marvel!"

"He's a mystery," Carolina said.

Turri's collection of illustrations was vast and far ranging. She thumbed through the lives of the saints, illuminated in heavy gold, blue, and red. She learned the types of American plants and vegetables, their blossoms precisely rendered, their roots perfectly free of earth. She traced the riggings of fifty renowned Spanish ships. She observed Africa's fantastic wildlife: lions, zebras, and giraffes. She furrowed her brow over chemicals and their combinations, and laughed at the constellations.

As the leaves turned bright and fell into the lake, the blindness pressed in. Now, looking out over the still water, she could see neither bank, only an ever-closing oval that contained the white faces of the last water lilies between the red bellies of the lily pads, curling up against the cold. Even in broad daylight she now moved in perpetual darkness. She could still see into the distance of her shrinking field of vision, but close at hand it was as if she carried only a small lantern, just powerful enough to reveal things directly in front of her.

Half blind, she became clumsy, bruising her white shins on Pietro's unfamiliar furniture.

"They are going to think I am beating you!" Pietro joked, when he discovered a new bruise. "But you are much too pretty for that."

To keep from losing her lake to the darkness, Carolina took planting sticks from the gardener to stake out the safest path. Over a period of days, she tied lengths of thick twine between them to lead her along, until her soft hands were nicked and chafed.

"You look like you have been doing smallwork for the devil," Pietro said.

Then, one night, Carolina knocked a clock from its place as Pietro led her from the dining room to the stairs.

The clock sat on a shelf just about the height of her elbow. The hall was wide enough that she should have been able to avoid it easily. But her vision had constricted so that it was impossible for her to see all the ornaments displayed in the hall and still find her own way.

The clock fell with an angry jangle of chimes. Springs and gears scattered everywhere. The beautiful white ceramic face with its hand-painted daisies seemed to be in one piece until she knelt to retrieve it, when it came apart as shards in her hands.

"Carolina!" Pietro said. "This was my grandmama's!"

There was no anger in his voice, only surprise and hurt. When he knelt beside her and began to scrabble helplessly among the pieces, he avoided her eyes. She realized with a deep pang that he believed she had broken the piece deliberately.

"No, no!" she said, catching his arm. Awkwardly, his powerful body yielded and turned toward her. Both of them crouched, balanced on the balls of their feet, unable to settle their knees amid the glass and machinery. "I couldn't see it, Pietro," she said, her eyes suddenly filled with tears. "I can't see!"

This was the first time he had ever seen her weep. The unstoppable river of his thoughts diverted for a moment around this new branch fallen into its path. He rose, lifting her with him.

"But it was right there," he said, reasoning slowly.

Carolina held her hands to each side of her face. "I cannot see my hands," she said. "I cannot see beyond them. It is worse every week."

"You cannot see," Pietro repeated.

"I told you," she said, begging. "I told you before we married."

After a moment, recognition sprang up in his eyes. "But you were joking!" he exclaimed.

When she didn't speak, he wrapped his arms around her, covering her eyes with one strong hand as he pressed her face to his chest.

The next morning, she awoke to find him leaning over her, shielding her eyes from the sunlight with his hand. The following evening, he scooped her up from her chair and carried her upstairs. "But there is nothing wrong with my feet!" she insisted.

For some reason, her blindness rekindled the fire in him that had begun to flicker after their return from the shore. Instead of retreating to his own rooms each night as he had been, he stayed with her or carried her to his. "Who is it?" he would whisper, covering her eyes with his hands, as if she had to guess. Or, "But I am a blind man!" he would protest, tangled in her garments as he searched for her flesh.

This lasted for a week. Around the lake, the trees gave up their last leaves. When their branches were black and bare, Pietro's ardor began to fade. He still reached for her when they met by chance, but he rarely sought her out.

Carolina, for her part, didn't miss him. Serving as the only audience for a man raised by crowds of admirers exhausted her. Soothing his distress over her blindness, while the darkness inched inexorably forward in her own eyes, was beyond her strength. The buried thought that he might have found comfort elsewhere was almost a comfort to her.

The night itself had become her favorite companion, the only one who seemed to understand what blindness meant. She no longer lit lamps or candles to hold it off: every night, she unfastened her buttons and clasps in full darkness. Especially after breaking the clock she didn't dare roam Pietro's unfamiliar house, but there was nothing to stop her from padding around the confines of her own room, searching out new mysteries: the sharp ceramic lace on a figurine's dress, the smooth bellies of a bowl of shells, the long, slick curves of her twin wardrobes.

When she did creep into her bed, she often pulled the sheets and blankets free and reversed them, with her pillows at the foot. If she tilted her chin from this position, what was left to her of the night sky filled her vision, the stars as bright as she could ever remember them, the borders of the moon still untouched by her collapsing sight.

"Maybe you are wrong about the New Year," Carolina said. She closed one eye and then the other, trying to recall which of the lake trees had stood at the limits of her vision the previous Sunday. "I don't think it is any different this week."

Turri skipped another silver disk across the lake's bright surface. Carolina turned her head quickly to keep it in sight before it skidded one final time and dropped into the depths.

"What are those?" she said, holding out her hand.

"They are blanks," he said, pressing one into her upturned palm. "For my mint."

"Your mint?"

"Last year I invented my own currency," he told her, a hint of derision in his voice.

"Because ours was not working?"

"Currency is the foundation of any new civilization," Turri said, as she imagined a professor might. "That, or an army. But coins are easier to produce in a laboratory."

"May I keep it?" she asked.

Turri flung another disk out into the lake without answering. Carolina dropped her head to work the unstamped coin into the slash of red satin at the waist of her dress. Then she looked up again to inspect the bare trees on the far banks. Their reflections shuddered in the wake from Turri's game.

"Or perhaps the trees are moving," she suggested.

"No, they are not," he said gently.

When the winter nights grew longer than the pale days, Carolina came downstairs to find Dr. Clementi standing alone in the front hall, nervously stroking the scuffed leather of his medicine bag. She had always liked the old man: unlike the other doctors in town, he had a strong sense of his own helplessness. In some acute cases, when he had reached the limits of his knowledge, he had been known to refuse to give diagnosis or treatment, despite the pleas of the patient, when his colleagues would cheerfully have tortured them to death.

Pietro, who hadn't informed her of the appointment in advance, was nowhere in sight.

"Dr. Clementi," Carolina said, greeting him midway down the stairs.

The old man squinted up through a pair of wire spectacles. When he recognized her, his face broke into a smile. "Hello, child."

"You're not here to see Pietro," she guessed, alighting from the last step.

He shook his head. "He's healthy as a horse."

"I think he's healthier than some horses," Carolina said, and gestured for him to follow her into the conservatory.

After some hesitation, the doctor settled on a prim, straight-backed chair, upholstered in red brocade. Carolina sank down on a divan near him. The doctor gazed at her in a visible agony over how to begin. His sympathy caused her more pain than any of her own thoughts had.

When it became clear that he couldn't bring himself to speak, she said, "I am going blind."

The doctor nodded, gratitude and sorrow struggling in the lines of his tired face.

At this moment, Pietro strode into the salon. "Doctor!" he said heartily. "I see you have discovered my wife. Thank you for coming."

The doctor held up bravely as Pietro thumped him on the back. Then Pietro sat down beside Carolina and took her hand without glancing at her. "Carolina is having some trouble," he said, confidentially.

"I see," the doctor said.

"I am going blind," Carolina repeated.

"It's like the darkness is closing in," Pietro elaborated. "She runs into things."

Dr. Clementi looked at Carolina with compassion, shadows threatening him from every side. "We thought you might have some medicine," Pietro said, prompting him. "Or a machine."

Dr. Clementi shook his head. "There is no medicine for it," he said.

"Or opium," Pietro insisted. "For the pain."

"There is no pain," Carolina said, laying her free hand over his.

"But there are remedies for weak eyes," Pietro said. "I have seen them."

Dr. Clementi, who now recognized his true patient, watched Pietro with pity. "I'm sorry," he said, and rose. "No doctor has ever arrested the progress of blindness."

"Thank you," Carolina said.

At the door, the doctor paused. "You have spoken with your parents?"

Carolina nodded. Even from that distance, and despite her failing sight, she could see he knew this was a lie.

"Cara mia," her father said. He looked into her eyes for a moment, then glanced aside, as someone might avert his gaze from the body of a bird fallen in the woods. Carolina closed her eyes in his embrace, comforted by the familiar smells of lemon and tobacco. When he released her, he turned to look out the large window, down the hill, where the glossy leaves of his groves glistened under the thin dusting of the first snow. Her mother watched her steadily.

Carolina had known the instant she opened their invitation for dinner that the old doctor had paid them a visit. Now she looked back at her mother, who seemed in danger of being snuffed out at any moment by the dark clouds that surrounded her. For the first time, she saw the fine lines in her mother's pale face, the lace at her neck, the shape of her dark eyes, instead of looking for an answer in them.

After a moment, her mother looked away. "After all, there is not really so much to see," she said.

"Can you see me?" Pietro whispered.

Thick winter clouds had hidden the sun all day, and now they blotted out the moon and stars. Since the cloud-bound night sky held nothing but more darkness, Carolina had pulled the curtains shut and settled into her bed as the maid had made it up, without turning the blankets and pillows so she could see the stars. Pietro's voice came from the doorway, but without the help of moonlight, Carolina couldn't distinguish his shadow from the general darkness. His question had woken her from a dream: a house had caught on fire in the snow, and the heat of the flames was melting the ice from the branches of the surrounding trees.

"No," she said, aloud.

Pietro stepped into her room, fumbled for the edge of her bed, and sat down on it. Blindly, his hand found the hollow of her neck, brushed her chin, and settled, open, on her cheek. With this as his guide, he kissed her deeply. He reeked of wine.

Then he laid his head on her chest, like a child. "I am so sorry," he said, his voice thick with tears, as if he were confessing some wrong against her.

As Christmas approached, the blindness advanced again, erasing all but the faces of her family and servants and the perfect circle of the full moon, tiny with distance. Her lake was reduced to bright patches of snow on the banks, a flash of silver reflected on the black surface, a rootless tangle of branches. She could no longer see enough of the sky to make out the weather by sight, and she found her way to and from the lake only with the help of the stakes and string she had tied together to guide her as autumn died.

"We're having a hailstorm," Turri told her, standing beside her on the banks of the lake. During the night, it had glazed over with a thin layer of clear ice, which shrieked and snapped now as it broke up under the weak sun. "The hail is as big as walnuts."

Carolina laughed. "I think I would feel that."

"Yes," Turri agreed. "But what you can't see is that I have erected, with the silence of a cat, a sturdy shelter over our heads. Surely you can hear the storm as it batters." A thunderous drumming accompanied this.

Carolina turned her head this way and that, scanning for a clue to the false hail as it echoed through the clearing. She saw the fabric of his walking-jacket, a window of her house, grass trampled in the clear slush under their feet, but he was too quick for her to catch.

At last, her gaze did settle on something she recognized: his blue eyes, laughing, the white sky overhead.

By the day of her father's Christmas party, the world was left to Carolina only in unreliable pieces. The darkness had completely overrun its borders. Now she could barely take in a whole face with a single glance. If she looked at their eyes, she lost the plaits and pearls in the hair of the girls, and even as they spoke, a shadow might pass over their features, obscuring their nose or mouth. From time to time, one glance might still be achingly sharp: the reflection of a bird, flying high over the water; the fire of an emerald on an old woman's hand. But more frequently the shadows crowded into even the brightest scenes, so that Carolina lived now in a permanent twilight that grew more like night each day.

Since before she was born, her father's family had hosted a feast in the week between Christmas and the New Year. This year, as always, the house was crowded with evergreen boughs, studded with lemons and fluted red flowers from her mother's hothouse. Garlands were fastened to the mantels, the doorways, the stairway railings with yards of shining gold ribbon. Wicks blazed

in every chandelier and lamp. Maids circulated through the crowd with great trays of
marzipan, fashioned into the shape of
lemons, grapes, apples, roses, tomatoes,
lions, lambs.

Carolina stood against the wall in the
ballroom, catching glimpses of her friends
and neighbors as they danced through
clouds of black smoke.

"Have we met before?" Turri asked, taking
advantage of the social requirements to kiss
her hand.

"I don't know," Carolina said. "Maybe
you can refresh my memory."

"It was at least a hundred years ago," Turri
said. "I had been wandering in the forest
for days. You were, as I recall, a little stream
unmarked on any map. I didn't mark you
on my own, thinking to keep you my secret,
but then I could never find my way back."

"I don't remember that," Carolina said.

"Or perhaps I was a sailor," Turri continued. "On the boat you took to Spain."

"I have never been to Spain," Carolina
said.

"You have," Turri said. "You used to lash
yourself to the mast, so you could watch the
storms. I was the one who untied you each
morning."

"I do like storms," Carolina conceded.

The heavy scent of almond mixed with the notes of a dozen perfumes: cinnamon, gardenia, orange and musk. Turri's fingertips alighted on the small of her back. "Would you like to dance?" he asked.

Carolina looked at him. "I can see only your face," she told him. "No dancers, no chandeliers."

"That's perfect," Turri said, pressing his palm flat against her back to lead her to the floor. When she resisted, he released her.

"Pietro," she said.

For a moment, Turri's face disappeared, replaced by the crescent of his ear as he turned his head. On the far wall beyond him, a lamp burned, interrupted by the shapes of dancers in their red and turquoise and furs. Then Turri's eyes, again.

"He is dancing," he said.

"With whom?" she asked.

Without answering, he led her into the crowd.

Carolina traced the ember as it rose into the sky and exploded, white sparks spinning far beyond the borders of her vision.

"You see it?" her father asked eagerly. *"Cara mia?"*

Carolina nodded at the sky.

"Yes?" her father asked. "That is a yes?"

"Yes," Carolina said.

At midnight, all their hardiest guests had assembled on the banks of her lake, where, from the opposite side, a pair of gypsies were shooting off a small fortune's worth of fireworks the seller claimed had traveled all the way from China.

Another firework: blue, dripping down the sky in long arcs like the branches of a willow. Red rockets reflected in the black surface of her lake, which rocked gently with the ripples some guest had made, throwing in a small stone or a last piece of marzipan. Yellow bursts seemed to turn to scattered gold on the snow below. Carolina caught all of this only in fragments, half seen, half imagined.

"Are you cold?" Pietro asked. Before Carolina could answer, he engulfed her in the folds of his own cloak, so that both of them were wrapped in the thick lengths of wool. Caught in his arms, she watched every temporary constellation blaze up and die out, even as the other guests began to drift back to the house for a bit of warmth or another glass of wine.

As the last one died, she continued to gaze up, her sight temporarily seared by the memory of the falling sparks even after the night sky went dark again, with the exception of the few remaining stars.

As Turri had promised, the New Year brought her complete darkness. The few scraps she had been able to see — the eyes of the servants, a fragment of horizon beyond her window — all dwindled down to unreadable points of light. Then one morning, she awoke to find that even those lights had gone out.

At first she believed she had simply woken early, and would have to wait for the sun to rise. But then she realized the house was alive with midday sounds: footsteps on the stairs and tramping on the roof overhead, perhaps removing a heavy snowfall so that the ceiling would not cave in. Outside children screamed and laughed.

Where am I? she thought, suddenly awash with horror. Immediately, her hands closed around the familiar covers of her bed, the pillows beneath her head, and, as she fumbled farther, the corner of her nightstand, the soft faces of her flowers, the sharp gilt flourishes that encased her clock.

She had not been able to see any of these things clearly for weeks, but with all light now lost, they suddenly seemed to be the only objects left to her in a living darkness that might well have consumed the rest of the world. For all she knew, she might be floating through dead stars far above an exploded world, and this might be the last moment her fingers would touch the table's smooth varnish before it drifted out of reach forever. She didn't dare call out: if she did, whatever had wreaked this disaster might turn back and finish the job by extinguishing her.

She could have lain like that for days, hands clenched around folds of velvet until hunger or fatigue pulled her down into a different sleep. But moments later footsteps padded up the stairs. They paused at the door, then entered without knocking. As their sound moved around the room, familiar shapes began to emerge from the gloom. Silk whispered as it rose from her floor and sighed faintly when put to rest in her wardrobe. Cut-glass bottles of perfumes and cream clanked gently. The panels of her curtains brushed the floor as they were drawn open. Wind poured through the window, bringing with it the memory of the long green slope of the yard. The wind was bitingly cold; Carolina's mind instantly stripped the summer trees of their leaves and blanketed the gardens with snow.

A terra-cotta jar scudded along the floor. Leaves and petals brushed together. Water splashed onto the roof beyond the open window, and new water poured evenly into the vase.

Then the footsteps ceased, only a few feet from Carolina's bed. The room went quiet. In the silence, the darkness rushed in again and stopped, seething, in the open door. Her bed, the clock, her familiar silken things held steady against it for the moment. But the other figure in her room was elusive: a pair of cloth slippers, an apron, a pale hand, fading into nothing where the person should have been.

"Who is it?" Carolina asked.

The footsteps turned and left the room without giving an answer.

"I will carry you," Pietro said.

Carolina shook her head.

"But it's been weeks since you've been downstairs."

"I can't see any difference."

"We'll make a fire. You'll feel the heat."

Carolina was seated on the damask stool before her vanity, where two mirrors flanked a greater one, reflecting her lost image at endless angles. For days — it might have been weeks — she had navigated the small room in perfect darkness, reclaiming its elements from the shadows one by one. Now she could sink onto her bed without first groping blindly for it. She could open the window, or close it. She could reach for a perfume as surely as if she could see. But she was not willing yet to go downstairs, where everything would be strange to her, to endure Pietro's sympathy and the curiosity of the servants.

Her eyes, although they couldn't see, still obeyed her in other ways. Now she lifted them to the mirror, near where Pietro's reflection should be.

Behind her, Pietro shifted uneasily.

"I would like to help you," he said.

Carolina rose, crossed the foot of her bed, and turned accurately to meet him by her night table. She lifted a rose from the glass, found his hand, and folded his fingers around the stem.

"Carolina —" he began.

"I am glad you came," she said.

Every day, Liza came to comb out Carolina's hair and pin it up again. One morning, long after Carolina had lost track of the days, she asked the girl, "Are you needed in the afternoons?"

"By who, ma'am?" Liza asked.

Carolina didn't know. "In the kitchen, or the — other rooms."

"Isobel serves in the evenings," Liza told her. "I usually go at noon."

A twist, a pin, a twist, a clip. Liza separated another length of hair from the rest and began to brush it.

"I would like you to bring me some books," Carolina said.

"What books?"

"The ones Signor Turri brought," Carolina said.

Liza pinned the final piece into place, exposing Carolina's bare neck.

"And I'll want you to stay with them," Carolina added.

When Liza returned that afternoon, Carolina was seated in one of the wing chairs that stood by the window at the foot of her bed. She had looked out of the same window a hundred times before, and she had a hundred memories of the line of pines that bounded the forest beyond it. But as she had tried to call them up to replace her lost sight, the memories had changed and faded. The strong trunks of the individual trees vanished. Their long needles softened into a haze. Sometimes an aspen, yellow with autumn, sprang up among them uninvited. Sometimes the entire line of pines was replaced by the trees that faced her father's property, which had had years to root in

119

her memory before she had ever seen Pietro's land. The harder she concentrated, the faster the forest in her mind shifted and was lost.

"I have brought the books," Liza said.

"Thank you," said Carolina.

In the doorway, Liza took a step back under Carolina's blind gaze.

"You may bring them here," Carolina told her.

For a moment there was silence. Then Liza crossed the room and came to a stop beside the chair opposite Carolina.

"Please, sit," Carolina said.

Liza obeyed.

"Which ones did you bring?" Carolina asked.

Leather brushed against binding fabric, and a book fell open.

"Maps," Liza answered.

"No," Carolina said. "What else?"

One set of pages slapped together. Another opened. "Birds," Liza said.

Carolina shook her head.

"Flowers and strange fruits," said Liza.

"Of Africa," Carolina said, naming the title from memory. "Flora and vegetation. Open that."

"There is a tree like a monster," Liza said.

"Good," Carolina said. "What else do you see?"

"Trees with monkeys."

"What kind of trees?"

"They have leaves like a fan, as long as my arm. They are shiny like varnish. This tree grows up and down. It has a hundred trunks. There is a man inside, between the trunks, standing up and looking out. This one is a flower."

"Like one of our flowers?"

"No," Liza said. "Like a lion roaring, with feathers for teeth. But his face is red, and his stripes are white. Here is a lily as tall as a child. It is yellow. The child is white."

"What is on the next page?"

"Next is a bird, with the face of a monkey."

This was a lie. The book had been one of Carolina's favorites, and boasted no such creature.

"No," Carolina said. "It is a jacaranda tree. It is silver with purple flowers, and it lines every street in the city."

Liza was silent.

"Go ahead," Carolina said, after a moment.

"It is a fruit," Liza said, finally. "With thorns like a rose."

For those first several weeks, the darkness

was complete. But then Carolina began to see again, in her dreams.

At first the glimpses were so slim they might only have been memories: the sun blazing through the new spring leaves, which seemed to be in danger of disintegrating in its rays; a box her mother kept by her bed, red cloth, embroidered with a white parrot; a silver bowl full of lemons. But then the stray images began to form themselves into events she knew had never happened. Her father lifted the lid from a basket of plums to find it guarded by a white asp with pink eyes. Pietro bounded out the front door and, with a laugh, rose into the sky.

It took her perhaps a week to sort the fragments of sleep from memory and recognize that she could see again in her dreams. As soon as she was certain, she began to make attempts to exert her will in the unreal world. Pietro could fly. Why shouldn't she? But flight didn't come to her instantly. She began simply by turning around. If she found herself walking up the stairs in a dream, she stopped, pivoted, and started down. Maybe she discovered herself in the midst of a game, but that didn't mean she had to play. As the men rolled the wooden balls over the grass, she slipped away and disappeared into the lemon grove, or lost herself in the forest. She might emerge from the woods again on a shell-paved road, or discover a new ocean lapping at the other side of the grove.

At dream parties in unfamiliar homes, she began to open doors, step backward through them, and close them behind herself before any of the other guests noticed. One door led her into a room filled with hundreds of white statues of human figures, no bigger than doves, set on small shelves in the high walls. Another opened into a clearing at the foot of a giant tree with the smooth skin of an elephant. Pale blue flowers had somehow found a way to blossom on its bark like moss. One time she stepped backward, not into a new room, but into a cold galaxy that she fell through endlessly, her heart seasick, her lungs aching with fear until at last she awoke, grateful for the moment to find herself in simple darkness.

Someone knocked on her door again, as implacable as the angel of death.

Carolina extricated herself from the embrace of sleep. She had no idea what time it was, or even what season. She pulled her covers over her chest and sat up.

"Yes?" she said.

The door opened.

"Your father is downstairs," Liza said. "It is three o'clock in the afternoon."

Carolina shook her head. She had not seen her father since her sight left her, and he had not sent any warning in advance.

"I am not dressed," Carolina said.

"They are waiting in the conservatory," Liza added.

Carolina bowed her head and pressed the heels of her hands against her eyes.

"I will help you," Liza said.

Carolina nodded and pushed the covers back.

In a few minutes, they had buttoned Carolina into a pale gold day dress and Liza had twisted and pinned Carolina's hair into place. A pair of pearl teardrops dangled from her ears, and a strand of pearls lay heavy on her throat.

"There you are," Liza said. Enamel scraped on glass as she set the brush down on the vanity.

Carolina rose and crossed to the door, where she stood for a moment, both hands pressed flat against her rib cage, as if holding it shut after a flock of birds had already flown out.

"Thank you," she said.

She made her way quickly down the main stairs. A few steps from the bottom, she caught the sound of voices from the conservatory, and stopped.

"Of course you could never have known," Pietro said gently.

"No," her father insisted, his voice wavering with tears. "God would not do this without warning. There was something I didn't see."

At the sound of her father's grief, Carolina turned and rushed back up the stairs. On the first landing, she collided with Liza. Carolina caught the girl by the wrist and pushed her back into the far corner, where they were hidden from view.

"Tell them you could not wake me," Carolina whispered fiercely.

Then, biting back her own tears, she caught her skirts together and slipped back up to her room.

In her dreams, Carolina tried to do two things: fly, and find her lake. The lake should have been easy to reach, especially from familiar terrain like Pietro's home or her father's lemon groves, where her dreams often began. But again and again, the lake was gone when she reached its location, replaced by a field of orange lilies, a grassy hill, a stand of ancient trees. Her house became a wind-burnt shell, or a woodsman's hut, or, once, a shop selling lace and candy.

She tried to fly a hundred different ways: jumping down a staircase; throwing herself from roofs, windows, and trees; flapping her arms and her skirts; running and leaping from the hard-packed dirt where the servants' children held their races. But finally she began to fly when she wasn't trying. Deep in a forest carpeted with black violets, she discovered herself rising from the path. She was already ten feet from the ground before she believed what was happening, and another story higher before she realized she couldn't stop rising. She caught the branches of a tree to keep from ascending helplessly into space and worked her way back down its trunk hand over hand. After a few experiments in its shelter, she learned enough of the new mechanics to sail between the sturdy trunks in fits and starts and to rise and dive as she wanted.

Those woods were real. She had visited them often as a child to gather flowers to throw into her lake so she could tell her fortune by the way they floated or sank. If her dream behaved, the lake should be only a short flight away. Trembling, Carolina let herself rise between the branches until she broke out of the canopy into the strong Italian sun. She dipped to prove to herself that she could return to earth, snatched one of the high leaves, and let it drop from her fingers as she rose higher, taking in a sweep of the fields and homes in her valley that was wider than anything she had ever seen.

Her father's house was as it should be, red tile and white stucco, flashes of statues in the garden, groves running down the slope in even rows. Pietro's house was there as well, with the long road leading by the pines. The Turri home shone on the next hill. She rose higher and caught sight of the river that fed her lake. The silver band cut a clear path between the trees, then disappeared just where it should have widened into the clearing.

Carolina glided lower, glancing over the countryside in case the lake had slipped in space, as things so often did in dreams. But it wasn't lurking beyond the next hill or lost in Pietro's back acres. She swooped down to the river and skimmed along the bright stream until the trees closed over her head.

There, just where it should have been, was her lake, hidden from the sky by a stand of massive plane trees that had taken root in the shallow water. Amid them, his face lost in the shadows, was a man. In water up to his waist, he swung a heavy axe against one tree's broad base.

In the yard, a crash and a shout, and she was awake.

It was the dead of night when Carolina ventured downstairs for the first time after going blind. She stood for some uncountable time in her open door, listening for any sign that everything beyond had not been erased by darkness. It was the scratching and cooing of the birds on the roof that gave her the courage to step out onto the soft carpet. From there, she simply turned and reached, as she had done a hundred times before, for the smooth support of the thick banister. It led her faithfully down the wide stairs and deposited her on another carpet in Pietro's main hall. Here, separated from the sound of the birds, her own steps muffled by the wool, the silence was so deep that the darkness rushed in, threatening to consume her. Instead of cowering before it, she threw her hand out and caught the knob of the front door. At this proof of the world's existence, the darkness retreated. She began to feel her way through the house.

She started at the borders of the rooms, her fingers trailing over smooth walls broken by cold windows. She spread her palms flat on brocade upholstery, trying to remember whether it was green or gold. She tangled with potted palms in the corners. The rough faces of the various portraits had nothing to say to her, but their frames were such a symphony for her fingertips that she wondered if the elaborate fashion hadn't been started, perhaps, by an unnamed artist for his blind wife, now long forgotten.

A few things had changed. All around the house unfamiliar candles had been scattered to hold back the winter gloom. For whatever reason, Pietro had ordered the piano dragged across the conservatory and the case propped open, even though neither of them played. "What are you doing here?" she whispered, touching the silent keys. Here and there, she found new figurines: a pair of tiny elephants, one's trunk relaxed, the other trumpeting; a new globe with raised continents; a small piece on the salon mantel, ceramic, full of spikes and smooth patches, which remained a mystery despite repeated visits.

Each night, she went a little farther. Eventually she began to strike out into the center of the rooms, navigating around remembered buffets and carts, sofas and tables. Pietro didn't have a library to speak of, but she pulled books down from his few shelves and sat with them on her knees, imagining the unseen pages now filled with heroic tales, now with verse, now with the histories of lost cities. She learned to enter the dining room and stride across it to her own chair. She found the cook's chocolate and flour, her onions, her vinegar. She entered the salon and threw the curtains wide to the night sky, then pulled them closed again.

For weeks, her explorations went on in perfect silence. Then, one night, she heard footsteps in the next room.

She froze. One hand closed on the heavy candlestick she had been examining. The footsteps had fallen in the main hall. She stood in the salon. When Carolina went still, the footsteps also stopped.

Carolina crossed the wide room and darted across the hall, into the conservatory. A quick touch revealed that the piano had not been moved from its new place, and that the case was still raised, forming a huge shadow that would hide her from the rest of the room. She took up a position beyond it and froze again, but the footsteps didn't follow. The house breathed normally. Then, rooms away, she heard a creak and a thud as a door swung open, and shut.

A few nights later, as Carolina was investigating the ever-changing fruits and vegetables on the kitchen counter, she caught the sound of the footsteps again when they stumbled into a chair in the dining room. Instantly, Carolina crossed to the swinging kitchen door and threw it open. She stood on the threshold between the rooms and held her breath so as not to miss the smallest sound. This time, the footsteps' escape was almost clean, except for a rustle of crumpled paper in the pantry where the girls trimmed and arranged the garden flowers.

The next night, the footsteps found Carolina in the conservatory, where she stood at the window fingering the neck of a violin that was naked of strings. Immediately, she set the instrument back into its case.

The footsteps ceased.

Carolina strode toward the last sound she'd heard, stepping neatly around the piano, a divan, and a low table.

The footsteps were not so lucky. In great confusion, they crashed into the door, dived through it, and stumbled into Pietro's office, a small room dominated by a pair of great desks whose surfaces were completely obscured by letters, contracts and circulars, tobacco plugs, bits of pencil, pots of ink, and brutalized pens.

Relentless, Carolina circled the close space, her open palms brushing the walls, the chairs, the faces of the desks. But from mercy or fear, she didn't pull the chairs away to reach under them.

Instead, she waited.

One by one, the dark minutes rolled after one another. Then the faintest of sounds: a scrape, a breath.

"I can hear you," Carolina said.

Then she turned and left.

Spring arrived by water. Rain tapped at her windows and capered on the roof. Ice melted into streams that trickled down the face of the house or dropped in long falls from the window ledges. The yard, which had been silent all winter, was suddenly alive with voices. The cook scolded the laundress, the boys, and the geese. The young men sang obscene songs that seemed to have hundreds of verses. The gardener chuckled at the children's clumsy attempts at cruelty.

Through the window, Carolina could feel the sun on her skin and mark its progress as the light climbed from the floor onto her bed, toyed with her fingers, brushed a cheek, then fell with its full weight over her body before it crept away each afternoon.

132

All winter, the weak sun and the moon had been one and the same to her. Neither was strong enough to dispel her sense that she always moved through the same long night. But now the sunlight divided her life back into days, and the constant sound of other human voices proved to her again and again that she was not, as her blindness sometimes whispered, the first person in the world.

And her heart, which she could have believed had been snuffed out along with her sight, began to stir. Still stiff with loss, it flinched from the threat of love, retreating immediately at the thought of her father's voice, Turri's questioning gaze, or the visits Pietro still made to her room each day. He arrived in the mornings, sometimes carrying her breakfast tray, and rattled on with idle gossip or small emergencies around the house until his limited collection of topics ran out. Finally, he would lapse into silence while Carolina searched for something to add, unnerved by the fact that he could be looking at her hands, or her face, or out the window, and she had no way to know it. Almost immediately, though, that unease would be overcome by her new and constant fear — that anything she could not hear might have disappeared. The fear was so strong that when Pietro fell silent for too long, she imagined him swallowed up by the same shadows that had taken her sight. At these moments, filled with remorse, she reached for him with an urgency that only confused and disturbed him. Love, in this uncharted darkness, was too much to ask. But under the touch of the spring sun, her heart did begin to yearn for old comforts.

A few weeks after the arrival of spring, while the rest of the house was sleeping, she descended the staircase and slipped out the front door. Night poured over her, heavy with dew and turned dirt, the sweet bite of tulips and hyacinth, the weight of the whole dark sky bent low to kiss the curve of the earth.

She pulled the door shut behind her and kicked off her slippers. Then she stepped onto the flagstone walkway, one foot on stone and one in wet grass. She walked this way for about twenty paces, until the path ended at the road that ran past Pietro's home, separating it from the pine forest beyond. Carolina listened for a moment, then darted across, stopping when her skirts brushed the tall grass on the opposite side. She reached for the stake that should have risen to the height of her hip, right at hand: the first of the sticks and string she had planted that fall to lead her back to her lake.

It wasn't there.

Carolina gave her head a little shake and set her jaw. Then she knelt in the dewy grass, her arms sweeping the soft new growth in wide arcs, like a child making an angel in the snow.

Still nothing. She crept farther, her knees printed with the impressions of sticks and grass, her gown and robe soaked. Luckless, she stood.

Then she strode, palms outstretched, into the darkness. After a few paces, her bare foot twisted on a piece of wood. When she bent to retrieve it, she felt the familiar gardener's string, tied with her own knot. She dropped the stake and fed the string through her fingers. Another post, unmoored, rose into her hands without resistance.

Tears welled in her eyes. She stepped forward unsteadily on the uneven ground, guided by the lengths of coarse string. A third loose stake rose from the earth, and a fourth. Both were muddy, and wet leaves clung to them. For all she knew, the line could have been dragged hundreds of feet from the path she had marked. But when she pulled on the next length of twine, it didn't yield.

"Please, please," she said aloud as she

went forward, following the thread. It ended at a fifth stake, still fixed in the wet earth. Carolina knelt, covered the damp wood with both her hands, and laid her forehead on her knuckles. Then she straightened and followed the string to the next stake, and the next, on through the forest.

The path she had marked had been clear in the fall, but winter and spring had crossed it with broken branches, washed parts of it away to shallow gulches, and filled others with deep puddles. By the time Carolina made her way through the woods and around the lake, her hands were bleeding and her feet were numb. Her wet robe clung to her legs and belly.

The string ran out at the last stake she had planted, on the water's edge directly below her cottage. She let go of the twine and stepped gingerly down the bank, where she squatted to rinse her hands in the freezing water. Then she stood and walked the few paces to her house by memory.

She awoke to a gentle touch on her cheek. It rested there for a moment, then began to trace the curve of her face to the corner of her eye. Smiling, she raised her hand to push it away. Her fingers fumbled against the heavy wings of a moth, which went

136

frantic with terror. For a moment, the insect's strange body beat against her eyelid before it came to its senses and rose out of reach. Too late, Carolina hid her face among the velvets, but fear drained quickly from her heart as the familiar room took shape around her in her mind: the fireplace still black with Christmas fire, the wooden chair at the small table, the square of light she could feel clearly, falling on her bare shoulder.

But a window must be broken, if the moth had flown in.

Carolina rose on her knees, located the windowsill — and found her investigation stopped short by one of her scarves, which had been pinned neatly into place. Not only that, but the window beyond the scrap of silk was open: she could hear the woods chatter and breathe beyond, and feel some small wind, more like a sigh than a breeze. It was impossible that her father hadn't shut the house for the winter. Who had opened it?

Toying with this mystery, she twisted back amid the velvets. At the foot of the couch, something crashed to the floor: a bowl, maybe, filled with marbles or shells, which skittered over the wooden floor all the way to the far corners.

Outside, from the lakeshore, a sharp voice called, "Who's there?"

Carolina laughed out loud. Then she pulled her blanket up over her bare chest. "Turri?" she said.

Moments later, steps rang on the cottage stairs. The door rattled.

"Have you been staying here all winter?" Carolina asked.

"I wish," Turri said.

He was the first person she had spoken to outside her home since she lost her sight. For a moment, shyness paralyzed her. Then she raised her eyes to what she guessed must be his face.

"I'm much taller than you think," Turri said. "That's the third button of my shirt."

Carolina lifted her eyes higher.

"My Roman nose," he said.

She smiled, and tried again.

"There," he said. He fell silent.

A chair scraped along the floor. "Is this what the string and sticks were for, then?" he asked.

She nodded. Again, silence. Nothing could tell her if he was staring into her blind eyes, or gazing out at the lake. She frowned.

"Your sight has gone?" he asked gently.

"It's like light," she said. "Moving beyond a heavy curtain. When it's dark, nothing."

"I thought so when you didn't come to the lake," Turri said. The chair creaked as he leaned forward, or back. "I wanted to send you something, but I couldn't think what to send."

"Liza has been telling me lies about the pictures in your books," Carolina told him.

"That's wonderful," Turri said. "You should have her tell you as many lies as she can. I, for instance, have been building a flying machine. So as not to alarm our neighbors, I only use it after dark. Since the snow melted, I have spent the night in half a dozen trees."

"I wish you would take me," Carolina said.

"It only seats one," Turri said. Then he relented: "But I could teach you how to fly it yourself."

Carolina shook her head and flattened her palms on the soft velvet.

Outside, perhaps from the other side of the lake, someone called her name.

Pietro. She realized again that she was naked.

Turri had already risen. "I'll be gone before he sees," he said, speaking low.

Then, silence. No step on the stairs, no click of the door, betrayed him, as if he really had risen through the roof in the grip of a flying machine.

"Carolina!" Pietro shouted again, closer now.

Hurried, solid footsteps crossed the damp grass and mounted the stairs. Pietro threw the door open. In a moment, his arms enveloped her, his hands cold, his breath hot, his chest and forehead wet. As he gathered her up, something smooth and round pressed into her ribs. Carolina reached for it and touched satin.

"You left your shoes," he said in explanation. "I brought them for you."

Without releasing her, he dropped the slippers on the floor beside the bed, then spread his hands wide over her bare flesh. He kissed both her cheeks and pressed her face to his neck. "A maid found them, but I came for you myself," he said.

"Thank you," Carolina murmured.

His breathing slowed and became deep. His hand tightened in her hair. He kissed the side of her face, her bare shoulders, the dust and salt in the hollow of her neck, and pushed her back into the pillows of her couch.

Before she and Pietro even emerged from the pines, Carolina could hear that all the servants had spilled out into the front yard. Children laughed and shrieked in the throes of some game. Women murmured to one another. Men barked orders and others refused them with equal force.

When the two of them stepped out of the forest, a great cry rose up and the crowd rushed close. Little hands pulled at her torn robe. Grown ones reached for her arms and waist and elbow. Like a stubborn horse, Carolina drew to a halt and turned her face against Pietro's chest.

Pietro laughed. "All right," he said. "Stand back. Nothing is wrong. We've just come from a walk."

The babble of voices around them rose with questions and protests, but the hands fell away, leaving only Pietro's. He had half carried her all the way from the lake, since her punished feet couldn't support her weight without pain. Now he led her across the lawn, up the stone walk, and into the house. The door shut out the sounds of the servants and the birds, leaving them in sudden silence.

Pietro took her hand and set it on the banister.

"You know where you are?" he asked.

She nodded.

Pietro lifted her hand again, this time to kiss it. "If you can walk through the woods," he said reasonably, "you will come down to dinner from now on."

"It is another butterfly," Liza said. "With wings like a tiger."

Over the course of the last hour, Liza had been relentlessly precise in her descriptions. Carolina, waiting for her to break into a fabrication, had been equally relentless in her demands.

"And the page after that?" she asked, again.

An almost indiscernible hesitation.

Carolina held her breath, as she had as a child, stalking the valley's half-tame rabbits across her lawn.

"This one is a giant moth," Liza said, and waited.

It was a lie. The next page, Carolina knew with certainty, contained illustrations of a pair of butterflies with mottled green wings and pale blue bellies, so that they were equally invisible resting on a leaf or rising into the sky.

"I remember that," Carolina said quickly.

"It is sitting on a man's shoulder." Then, with a certain pride of authorship: "It is as big as his head."

"What color is it?" Carolina asked.

"It has black-and-white eyes on each wing. They are slanted like a cat's. The wing tips are orange," Liza added with relish.

"That one was very beautiful," Carolina said, feigning wistfulness. "What is it called?"

"A giant cloudless emperor," Liza said with authority.

"And on the next page?" Carolina asked.

"It is another giant," Liza said, her bent toward deceit momentarily outstripping her imagination. "This one is carrying off an apple," she continued, recovering. "It seems to have picked it from a tree."

"I think there was a whole section of giants there," Carolina said, to prompt her.

"There are three of them," Liza agreed. "They are picking all kinds of fruits from an orchard. Lemons, apples, and plums. They are all blue, but one of them is bluer than the others."

"And on the next page?" Carolina asked.

"They are butterflies the size of birds. They are landing on the statues in a square. You cannot see the ground for their wings. Each wing has an eye and they are all looking back at me."

"I wonder what we would do if they landed around the house?" Carolina asked.

"We would pour oil on the grass and set it on fire," Liza replied matter-of-factly.

Carolina let that picture flicker in her

mind for a moment, a wave of giant butterflies rising out of low flames.

"And on the next page?" she said.

"It is a tree in a forest," Liza said, looking down at a page Carolina knew contained a portrait of a butterfly's bulb-eyed, monster's face, drawn ten times its actual size, with the enormous patterns of its gold-and-red wings spread like expensive wallpaper behind it. "But I don't see any creature. No, here. They are very small, covering the trunk like mildew. Some of them might be missing wings."

"And on the next page?" Carolina asked, again.

"Are there ghosts in this house?" Carolina asked.

Pietro laughed. A fire roared in the salon grate, but one window was open to the spring afternoon. Scents of hyacinth, rain, and manure drifted through. Attracted by the fire's crackle, Pietro had come to investigate, discovered his wife, and sat down with her on the couch that faced the wide mouth of the fireplace. He had caught both of her hands in one of his and was toying with her fingers on his leg.

"Maybe of the little dog I had to kill, after the horse kicked it in the head," he said. "I only hit his foot the first time, and had to shoot him again."

"I hear footsteps at night," she said.

"The servants are always working," he said.

"Not like this," Carolina insisted. "They won't answer when I speak to them."

"Maybe you have caught our thief," he said. "Someone has been stealing the lemon liqueur."

"I don't think so," Carolina said.

Pietro loosed her hands so that he could gather her up in his arms. He pulled her into his lap and kissed her.

"You are so beautiful," he murmured. "Who cares if you can see?"

"He has sent you a dress," Liza announced from the doorway of Carolina's room.

"Pietro?" Carolina asked. She twisted on the seat at her dressing table, where she had been turning over pieces of her jewelry in her hands: the smooth enamel, the cool metal, the jagged peaks of the diamonds and the rough clusters of gems in their settings.

Without answering, Liza flung the gown down on the bed in a great swoon of lace and fabric.

Carolina rose and bent over to collect the

dress. It was made of thin, stiff taffeta, the bodice reinforced with boning. Lace circled the low-cut neck and decorated the cap sleeves. The skirt fell away into numberless layers.

"It seems fine," Carolina said. "What color is it?"

"Gold," Liza answered. Then a short pause, long enough to repent of the truth — or a lie. "No, I am wrong. It is blue, with red lace."

"That is enough, thank you," Carolina said.

"You will see," Pietro said. "With the music and the dancing, I think you will be happy."

"It is a blue dress?" Carolina asked.

"It is a red dress," he said. "Red like wine in a glass. But the lace is blue."

Carolina frowned.

"Did you want a blue dress?" he asked. "That is easy enough to do. You can have ten of them if you want. But I don't know why the color should matter to you."

When she didn't answer, he laughed at his own joke. In a crowd, others might have joined in out of pity for him, but they were the only two in her room.

As the sound of his laughter faded, he took his wife in his arms and stroked her head. "Ah, Carolina," he said. "I never know what to do."

The dance was hosted by the Rossi family, which owned one of the oldest villas in the valley. Every Rossi was quick to boast that this stone floor had been laid, or that thick wall had been raised, during the time of the Romans, but they never seemed to be in agreement about exactly which wall or floor. No one doubted the great age of their home, however, because it was such an unholy mess of architectural experiments. Great marble pillars in the classical style jutted into the sky, supporting nothing; beautiful stonework was slathered with cheap stucco; a small army of coy nymphs beckoned all the way up the drive, where a pair of forbidding tigers, twice as tall as any man, frowned down on the arriving guests.

Atop a hill at the back of their property was a Gothic chapel whose roof had now collapsed, and in this generation, the Rossis had developed the habit of hosting their parties in it. The setting made a spectacular dance floor, exposed to the stars but sheltered by the surviving walls. Torches lit to illuminate the dancers found out the fragments of stained glass that remained in the old windows and made them glow.

Halfway up the hundred stone steps that led to the ruined chapel, Carolina stumbled for the second time.

"All right," Pietro said, steadying her with a laugh. "Maybe I should just carry you on my back."

Carolina shook her head and started off again, treading recklessly up the uneven stairs, following the music into the darkness.

In a moment, his hand caught her arm again. "Slow down," he said. "We are almost there."

Carolina knew that already from the sound of the instruments and the volume of the laughter. She could smell burning oil, wine, and traces of a dozen perfumes, along with the thick scent of tulips, which must, she guessed, be massed by the hundreds at the entrance.

"Carolina!" Contessa Rossi exclaimed. "My darling! We have not seen you for a year!"

"It hasn't been a year," Carolina said, surrendering her hand to the old woman's grasp.

Contessa Rossi's cold, insistent hands seemed to check that all Carolina's fingers were still intact, then released her. Carolina felt something pass before her face once, and again.

"She cannot even see that?" Contessa Rossi said to Pietro in amazement.

"My wife is not a toy for you to play with," Pietro said curtly.

"I suppose she is no one's toy but yours," Contessa Rossi said with a sly laugh.

"This is a beautiful night," Pietro said. "We are so grateful for your invitation." He bowed briefly, and led Carolina in.

"You will be happy by the music?" Pietro asked, his voice raised slightly over the strains of the dance.

Carolina nodded.

"Here is a seat." He pushed her back a few short steps until her calves pressed against a chair. Carolina sank into it. Its delicate arms were upholstered in brocade.

"What color is it?" she asked.

"What?" Pietro said, confused.

"The chair," she said. "What color is it?"

"It is gold," he said. "With some black threads."

"Thank you," Carolina said.

Similar chairs seemed to be arranged on either side of her, she discovered, but Pietro didn't take either of them. "Would you like me to bring you anything?" he asked.

She shook her head.

■ ■ ■ ■

Pietro had left her just steps from the dance floor, with the small band of musicians playing on her left. Carolina had not heard music since she went blind, and the effect was overwhelming. Her skin tingled from the violins. Her heart seemed to beat with each stroke of the cello, and the winds left her breathless. Forgetting herself, she closed her eyes. In her mind, the hill fell away below her feet and the musicians, the chapel walls, and the imagined dancers all rose gently into the black sky, as if suspended on glass in the heavens. Was this a dream, she wondered, or some other thing?

"Carolina!" A woman's voice: one she'd heard before, but didn't know instantly. "It's Sophia. You haven't forgotten me?"

Carolina opened her eyes to greet Turri's wife, guessing at the location of Sophia's face by her voice.

"Oh!" Sophia said.

Carolina smiled and held her gaze steady.

Sophia's recovery was swift. "I had to come give you a compliment on your beautiful dress," she said. "Don't you love the new year's fashion?"

"Thank you," Carolina said. "But I'm

afraid I didn't choose it."

"Oh, of course not," Sophia said. "I'm sorry. How thoughtless." A rustle of fine cloth and lace settled into the chair beside Carolina. Sophia took her hand. "How is it," she asked with elaborate sympathy, "to dress without sight, not to know whether a thing flatters you, or what you look like?"

Carolina squeezed her hand and released it. "My husband tells me I am beautiful."

Sophia laughed as if Carolina had just revealed herself to be surprisingly clever, for a child. "Of course he must say so," she said. "But how do you *know?*"

"Sophia, there you are," Turri broke in. "Princess Bianchi has been looking for you."

"But I just spoke with her."

"The woman is adamant," Turri said, an edge in his voice that Carolina didn't recognize.

Without another word, Sophia rose. Her skirts swung haughtily for a few steps, then were lost in the chatter and hum of the crowd.

Turri took Carolina's hand and held it for a moment. Then he kissed her fingers and settled into the seat his wife had left.

"Everyone is wearing plaster masks tonight," he said. "It's the new rage. They're not just for Carnevale anymore. I'm sur-

151

prised Pietro didn't order you one."

Carolina smiled.

"My wife, for instance," he continued, "is wearing a chicken's head that cost me ten thousand lire."

"Are the chicken heads the most stylish, then?" Carolina asked.

"I am not the man to answer that question," Turri said. "Clowns," he added after a moment, as if watching a pair pass by. "A cat."

In the background, Carolina caught her husband's voice, approaching. He stopped several paces away and laughed, overloud, as she'd often heard him laugh in the company of pretty girls. Then his voice dropped into conspiratorial tones and disappeared below the music.

"Contessa Rossi," Carolina said. "Is she wearing the new fashion?"

"Contessa Rossi," Turri replied, "is a hungry wolf in a Milanese dress."

A warm hand settled on the back of her neck. Carolina started and shrugged it off, but under his touch her flesh had come alive, singing and clamoring. Turri had never touched her like this before, and she couldn't understand why he would now. She struggled to keep her composure as heat beat through her in time with the music.

Pietro laughed. Instantly she realized: it had been his touch, not Turri's.

"Turri," Pietro said. He replaced his hand on Carolina's neck. "You didn't give me away."

"I'm afraid not," Turri said.

"Did you take me for a stranger?" Pietro asked Carolina, and bent to kiss the side of her face.

"I'm afraid not," Turri repeated low, speaking to himself. Another realization broke in on Carolina: Turri knew she had confused the two of them. He had seen her shake off the hand she thought was his.

"You surprised me," Carolina told her husband, to cover Turri's words.

"I was introduced to Princess Bianchi," he said. "She is visiting from Florence."

"She's very pretty," Carolina said.

"How did you know that?" Pietro asked in alarm.

Turri laughed and rose. "I had just asked your wife to dance," he said. "Do you object if she accepts?"

"She can't see your hand in front of her face," Pietro warned him.

Carolina rose as well. "I can hear the music and follow the steps," she said.

Maybe Turri waited for a sign of agreement from Pietro. She would never know.

After a moment, Turri touched the small of her back and guided her to the dance floor.

"I learned how to dance from a bear," Turri told her.

She laughed into what she thought might be his eyes.

His grip on her tightened. He pressed his cheek against hers, his lips at her ear. "What do you *see*?" he whispered, urgent but without hope, as if pleading with one of the old gods for a kind of mercy they had never shown.

Breathless, Carolina struggled against him.

"All right," he said, letting her go. "You will forgive me."

Carolina's skin was aflame. Blood beat in her temples louder than the music, and she felt dangerously weightless, as if only Turri's hands kept her from rising slowly into the atmosphere.

"Carolina?" he asked.

When she looked up at him again, tears stood in her eyes.

"No, no," he said. "They already think I'm a monster. Don't give them proof of it."

She laughed and a tear escaped down her cheek. In an instant, he had erased its track with his thumb.

"You will come meet me," he said. "At

the lake. When?"

"Tomorrow," she whispered.

Outside, the clatter of their carriage faded toward the stables. Pietro lingered for a moment, fumbling with something at the door. But as Carolina ascended the first few steps, he caught her hand.

"You like the dress?" he asked.

Carolina nodded. Then, realizing he couldn't see her in the darkness, she spoke: "Yes."

He kissed her palm, and her wrist. Following the line of her arm, he climbed the stairs until his mouth found the lace where her dress met her breast. With a sigh and a shudder, he lifted her into his arms and carried her up to her room.

Carolina awoke to the sound of a step outside her closed door. She turned her head and waited, as she so often had before, for shapes to emerge from the darkness. When none did, she pushed her hair away from her face and raised herself on her elbows.

Silence.

Then, although she heard no footfall, a board beyond the door creaked: a long groan, like a good soldier with a mortal wound giving his last warning.

"Pietro!" Carolina whispered, very low, so as not to frighten the unknown visitor. "Do you hear it?"

Pietro didn't stir.

A hand turned the doorknob slowly, with only the faintest clank and scrape of metal on metal. Carolina realized with a chill that if she were not already awake, the footsteps would be entering undetected. But the footsteps didn't enter. Instead, they waited as the door swung wide. Then, making no attempt at concealment, they walked away, unhurried and confident.

Long after they vanished, Carolina held still as a cornered animal, her fists balled in fury, as if she were the intruder in her own room.

When she woke again, Pietro was gone.

Outside, no birds sang and no servants complained.

Carolina rose at once and went to her dressing table. Naked in the darkness, she sorted through her jewelry box until she found her pearl earrings. She put them on, fastened the matching necklace around her neck, and went to her closet.

There, she chose a hunting dress with cotton lace at the elbows and bodice. She fastened it up expertly, then returned to her dressing table to pull her hair back in a quick knot. Her leather boots stood beside the closet. She threw a short cloak over her shoulders, cradled the boots in her arms, and descended the staircase barefoot. When she reached the front hall, she sat on the lower steps to pull the boots on and tie them. Then she crossed to the door and caught the knob.

It was locked.

Carolina twisted and pulled, but the door didn't budge. She pressed both palms flat against the cracked varnish, then ran her hands over the entire surface, the angles and planes of the deep rectangles that had been cut in the old wood. She traced down the narrow gullies where the door met the frame, searching for another latch to turn, a forgotten key.

Nothing.

In the yard, a dove cooed experimentally. Another answered. Soon the two of them were arguing, each repeating its own points word for word with increasing volume. After a few moments, a lark began to scold them. Suddenly, the whole morning was alive with birdsongs, obliterating one another and Carolina's thoughts.

In the back of the house, a door slammed.

Carolina gave the door a final pull. It held fast.

Without missing a step, Carolina returned to the stairs. She laid her hand on the railing as surely as if she could see it through the scattering darkness, and climbed back up to her room.

"I'll want a pen and ink," Carolina said that morning as Liza fastened a chain at the back of her neck. Liza dropped the clasp lightly onto Carolina's flesh and stepped away.

Carolina listened closely, to see if she recognized the step, but Liza was like a cat: Carolina didn't catch another sound until the girl had almost reached the door, when a board gave her away with a faint creak.

"Liza," Carolina said.

She had hoped to gauge the girl's position by her answer, but Liza didn't speak.

"Paper," Carolina added after a moment. "And wax and a flame."

Liza made no sound of assent, but after another moment Carolina knew with certainty that she had gone, as she still knew with certainty when daylight left a room.

When Liza returned, Carolina was already seated at the small writing desk on which Pietro's mother had once copied out the poems and composed the sentences of her own incomplete education. The desk sat at the window between the two wing chairs Liza and Carolina sat in to read.

Without ceremony, Liza deposited the objects on the thick paper mat that protected the fine wood. Something rolled: the pen. Carolina caught it before Liza did.

"The flame?" Carolina asked.

"I put it at the back," Liza said. "Reach out your hand."

Her palm flat, her fingers spread on the surface of the desk, Carolina investigated until she discovered the cold metal plate with its curled handle, the stalk of the candle securely fastened in the center. Liza had placed it at the far edge of the desk, just inches from the window. If it had been night, the light would have been evident for miles.

"You may close the door when you go," Carolina said.

As the door thudded shut, Carolina covered her collection of tools with both hands. She laid the stick of wax at the top of the mat, parallel with the line of the desk, like a dessert fork laid lengthwise above a dinner plate. She set the small heavy seal just above it. The glass bottle of ink she placed to her right, beside the pen. She set the paper to her left, then laid a single sheet down in front of her to write on. She lifted the glass stopper from the inkwell. In order not to lose track of it, she put the stopper in the glass trumpet that sprouted from the side of the well to hold the pen between thoughts so that the inked nib didn't stain the page. By this time, she no longer remembered the exact location of the paper. To remind herself, she found the top border of the page with her index fingers and ran them lightly out to the corners and down the sides of the sheet. Then she picked up the pen and dipped it in the ink.

As she raised the pen to write, a heavy drop fell on the desk. Carolina moved to set the pen back in the glass, but the stopper was in its place. Instead, she set the nib on the cusp of the inkwell just above the deep pool of ink, the length of the pen jutting up. Now she could only guess where the drop had fallen. She walked the fingers of one hand like a spider over the desk until her thumb found a small puddle. With her other hand, she pulled a handkerchief from her bodice and wiped the drop away. Then she reached for the pen again, but her motion was imprecise. The pen dropped into the well, submerging the entire nib in ink. Carolina retrieved it. Then, to prevent further spills, she carefully dragged the inkwell across the desk so the small bottle rested at the edge of the unwritten letter.

All morning Carolina's heart had been clogged with phrases and thoughts, incomplete confessions, pleas for help. She had begun a hundred sentences only to see them break apart in a flood of feelings her young mind could barely distinguish from one another: tenderness or desire, rage or fear, gratitude and love. But in her struggle with the pen and paper, all of that had gone. Hot with shame, she only wrote, in letters that she knew must seem ill-formed and childish, *"Your Carolina."*

Slightly dizzy from the smell of the ink, she waited for the letter to dry. Then she folded the paper into thirds and picked up the stub of sealing wax. With one hand, she grasped the root of the candle. With the other, she pressed the burnt wick of the sealing wax against the candle's smooth curve. Using the candle as a guide, she lifted the wax until one wick met the other and the sealing wax flamed up with a small hiss and a tiny gust of wind.

She fumbled again for the lifted flap of the letter, found it, and pressed it flat. Then she tilted the burning wax to seal it.

No drops fell.

Carolina turned the sealing stick upright and counted again, waiting for the dark wax to melt and pool below the flame. A moment later, searing heat splashed over her knuckles. With a short cry, she dropped the stub and began to blow frantically to snuff out the invisible flame. Moments later, her fingers found the stick again, the wick still hot, but unlit. Flecks of wax covered the desk and dotted the face of her letter.

Stubbornly, Carolina repeated her procedure, lit the wax, and held it over the raw edge of the paper. This time a stream of hot sealant poured evenly into place. Carolina blew out the second flame and laid the stub down. Then she pressed her own finger into the warm pool to seal the letter.

Her knuckles still burned. She stood, leaving the mess of ink and wax, and crossed the room to lay the letter on the table beside her bed. Then she rang for Liza.

Liza laughed. "It looks like you killed a cat," she said. "A cat with ink for blood."

"You may take it all away," Carolina said. "Scrape the wax and bring me another mat. And I'll want one of the boys from the stables."

"You're going riding?" Liza asked.

When the boy arrived, Carolina sat on the

edge of her bed, her burnt hand submerged in the pitcher of water from her night table. In the other, she held the letter.

The boy stopped at the door and indulged in a long moment of silence, to observe her, to collect his thoughts, or perhaps because he was young enough to believe he could not be heard until he spoke.

"Giovanni," he finally announced, with the frighteningly perfect mimicry of a child aping a man. From the timbre of his voice, the boy could not be much older than ten or eleven, but he spoke like a commander of numberless forces.

"Giovanni," Carolina repeated. "Thank you for coming. Do you know the Turri house? Up the hill, on the way to town?"

"I'm not afraid of lions," the boy averred. "Or dogs."

Carolina extended the letter to him, which made him feel the need for some gallantry. "You look very pretty this morning," he told her.

"How fast do you think you can run there?" she asked.

Because she kept her hands hidden below the tablecloth, Pietro did not notice them until dessert. When he did, he laughed.

"You look like you have been extracting

163

the ink from a squid," he said. "You know, we have girls who can do that for you."

He took her hand up to examine it. The heat of the fire still throbbed in her fingers, as it had all day.

"What's this?" Pietro said, alarm darkening his voice. "Have you cut yourself?"

"It's not a cut," Carolina said, reclaiming her hand. "It's a burn."

Silver clinked on china.

She waited for another barb or an outburst, but instead he just lifted her hand and kissed it, finger by finger.

"It is a fish shaped like a star, with five eyes like blue diamonds," Liza embellished. Over weeks of long afternoons, she had begun to understand that it was her lies, not her powers of observation, that were in demand when Carolina asked her to read. Whether out of distaste for other work or the joy of creation, she had begun to invent with abandon. Today she worked from a book containing specimens of the ocean's watery treasures.

"It is a silver tree that bends with the currents and drops fruit on the bottom of the sea."

"The fruit was red, wasn't it?" Carolina said, as if she remembered.

164

"No," Liza said, with an author's jealousy. "Purple like a plum, with silver on it, like breath on a glass."

"I thought there was a monster next," Carolina said.

"It is a monster," Liza relented. "It has two faces, one like a man, and one like a horse, with the body of a fish." This was elaborate, even for her, and presented as a kind of gift. Liza continued: "There is a bridle in its mouth, and a saddle on its back."

"Who do you think rides it?" Carolina asked.

Liza had not considered this implication of her invention. "It doesn't say," she said.

"There are no footprints leading away, in the sand at the bottom?" Carolina pressed.

Liza went silent, then decided to solve this new problem by eliminating its source. "You can't see the bottom," she said. "There is nothing but green water, until it goes black in the distance."

Footsteps approached the door of Carolina's room and stopped just beyond the threshold.

"Who is that?" Carolina asked sharply.

Liza let the pages of the book slap together and stood. "It's probably Giovanni," she said. "He's afraid to knock."

"Open the door," Carolina ordered.

Liza rose and crossed the room obediently. The door swung open. "Giovanni," Liza said. "It's not nice to stand outside a door."

"I was thinking," he said defensively.

"You can do that in the yard," Liza said.

"There is a man in the conservatory to see you," Giovanni told Carolina, and fled. His steps clattered down the stairs.

"He thinks he's in love with you," Liza said. "He tells all the other boys how pretty you are, and if they agree, he fights them."

"Thank you," Carolina said. "You may go."

A few steps from the bottom of the stairs, Carolina stopped. She knew without a doubt that it was Turri who waited for her, and she had come this far with the eagerness of a child about to reach home. But now her mind rang with a warning, as if on the last step she had stumbled into the world of spirits and overheard their gossip. She couldn't understand the words, but their meaning was clear: if she continued down the stairs, everything would change as completely as it had when her sight left her. For a moment, the premonition kept her in place. Then the cares of the world swept in

166

with their compelling arguments. She was standing like a fool in the middle of the staircase; there was a visitor waiting. Quickly, she descended the last steps and went into the conservatory.

Silence greeted her. She listened for a breath or a movement, but caught nothing. Uncertain, her fingers closed on the folds of her dress. Turri would never have made her wait so long.

"Who is it?" she demanded.

In answer, a long, low note echoed from the belly of a cello somewhere near the piano. As it faded, a man laughed.

"You don't know me," he said. "But maybe you have heard me play. Your husband took my card at the Rossi party and asked me to come some afternoons, in case you might like music."

His voice was full of gravel: an old man's.

"I do like music," Carolina said. Surprise had made her uncertain of everything. She reached out with both hands and found the doorway on either side of her just where it had always been. Marking her position by it, she stepped into the room and took a seat in the corner of the nearest couch. "I'm Carolina," she said.

"Silvio," the old man told her. A stroke, another note, and a song broke forth: fire licked at a single stick before the pile burst into flames, then a moment spent near dark water before the opening theme broke open again in variations as inevitable and unfamiliar as the speech of angels.

When it came to a close, she could hear the tip of the bow come to rest gently on the floor.

"Another?" the old man asked.

"Yes, please," said Carolina.

In her dreams, the flat roof of the Turri house was covered with white shells, despite the fact that she had never been on the Turris' roof in waking life, and that the cost of importing those shells from the coast would have been enormous. However improbable, the effect was striking. No matter how high she climbed, the white cross formed by the house's four wings stood out like a beacon among the gold roads and the dark heads of the trees. The ghostly shape was even visible at night, illuminated by the moon, as it was now.

Carolina wheeled through the night sky over Turri's house and grounds. Only one light still burned in the Turri home, on the second floor. She flew low over the back garden, then rose until she hung even with the lit window in the darkness.

Inside was a laboratory and workshop. Turri sat at a desk that faced the window, his head bowed over some complicated mechanism. To his right a small balcony jutted out from the house. It communicated with the laboratory by a narrow glass door. Carolina alit and tried the handle.

It opened so silently that for a sickening moment she wondered if she had gone deaf as well. Then she heard the scrape of metal against metal and a rhythm of clicks and clacks as Turri tested the machine on the table before him. He didn't look up when she entered, and Carolina didn't disturb him with a greeting.

Instead, she slipped past him to explore the workshop. The space was vast: only ten paces across, but so deep that the far wall was lost in darkness. The area where Turri worked was brightly lit by tiny gaslight fixtures set in the ceiling every few paces. To the left were glass cupboards filled with boxed specimens of moths and insects, as well as tall containers full of feathers carefully sorted by color: black, blue, brown, white, red, and a small unbound sheaf of green. A black marble counter, streaked with quartz and flaked with shiny mica, supported a small forest of boiling beakers mysteriously linked by lengths of thin yellow tubing. Steam billowed from each beaker, giving off the scent of anise, lemon, and iodine. Beyond the counter were shelves of jars filled with strange fruit, lengths of thick roots, unborn animals, birds without feathers. All these specimens had lost their true colors and taken on the faint blue of the thick liquid that suspended them.

Opposite the jars were books. Treading carefully, as though afraid to wake Turri, Carolina crossed the short span of glossy floorboards to read their titles: *Successful Flying Machines; New Italian Chemistry; A History of Tears; Five Thousand Constellations with Lost Stars.* In the lower corner of the bookcase, more than a dozen oversized volumes were missing — perhaps the ones he had chosen to send to her. In the shadows where they should have been, tiny lights glimmered. When Carolina peered closer, she discovered a globe: blue gone black in the dim light, marked with lines of dusky gold that traced the shape of constellations between the false stars. Somehow, the stars glowed from within, surrounded by halos of midnight blue where the light illuminated the dark surface. When she touched it, she realized it was made of paper, stretched tight over a wire frame, each star carefully punched out by hand. The back of the globe seemed to shed more light than the front, casting strange shadows in the bookshelf's deepest recesses. Curious, Carolina turned the sphere gently on its stand. A small tear split the globe, from the breast of a dragon to the horns of a bull. Inside, she could see the faltering shape of a naked flame.

Gently, she turned the globe to hide the tear. Then she walked back to where Turri still sat. He frowned as he pressed a silver lever that lifted a hammer to ring a small bell. Her skirts rustled, but he paid no notice. Carolina stood at his side as he pressed the lever again, swore softly, then tapped at the bell with his finger. It gave a muted peal.

Blood singing in her ears, she laid a hand on his shoulder.

Before he looked up, she awoke.

For days, Carolina expected Turri at every moment. Any sound might mark his arrival: a footstep outside her room; a servant running to the front door; the thud of a small bird, transfixed by her window. One morning the rooftop doves woke her with their cooing, and for several minutes, still in the throes of a half dream, she was convinced that he had crawled up into the eaves and was trying to speak to her in some new code. These hopes came unbidden, despite all her attempts to despair. She reminded herself of his failed experiments, the derision his name inspired, his unpredictability and his nonsense. She rehearsed the stories she had heard, of how slight a wind can snuff out a man's love. It made no difference. Her heart had been convinced by some secret math.

Pietro, in the brief hour they spent together over dinner each evening, seemed to see none of this. He reported on the progress of the vineyards and complained about the vintner. Until this summer, Pietro had taken no interest at all in his father's winery, so the old man had grown used to working his dark magic in perfect freedom. Now he responded to Pietro's presence with suspicion and his questions with exasperation. After a few weeks of tramping cheerfully through the rows of grapes and inspecting the copper tubs where the new wine brooded, Pietro had begun to offer suggestions. The old vintner was speechless with rage. Since the old man seemed unwilling to reason, Pietro tried reissuing his ideas as orders. This resulted in a complete breakdown in negotiations, after which the old man responded to anything Pietro said with a single word: *impossible.*

"He acts like the whole vineyard is planted in gunpowder," Pietro told Carolina. "And if we cut the wrong vine it will blow us all to kingdom come."

In the meantime, the front door remained locked. At first she thought it was only a passing fancy that led him to turn and take the key on the evening of the Rossi party. But as the days wore on, the old knob still refused to budge, not just at night, but by day as well. Carolina listened to Pietro's evening soliloquies with growing amazement, trying to understand how this genial, simple man could double as her jailer.

Finally, she asked.

"I wanted to go to the lake today," she said one evening, after a long disquisition on the merits of various grapes that even Carolina could tell Pietro had hopelessly scrambled. "But the door was locked."

"Yes," Pietro said agreeably.

Carolina laid her knife along her plate and lifted her eyes to his face. "I think I'd like to have a key," she told him.

His hand covered hers on the rough lace tablecloth. "It's not safe for you to go alone," he said.

When she didn't answer, he lifted his hand to her cheek, traced the curve of her chin, then leaned in to kiss it, and asked, "What

173

does it matter where you are, if you can't see?"

"A man is here," Giovanni announced from the doorway of Carolina's room, with an air of betrayal.

"Thank you, Giovanni," she said, wondering as she rose from her chair how the child could possibly have conceived a jealousy of the old cellist.

She stopped just short of the threshold, because she hadn't heard his retreating footsteps. As she had guessed, Giovanni still waited in the doorway.

"I could take your arm to help you with the steps," he suggested.

Carolina smiled at him with what she hoped was some accuracy. "I walk up and down the stairs every day," she said.

"But what if someone is hiding on them?" he asked. "Or a glass that fell from a tray?"

"I will be very careful," Carolina promised. "Thank you, Giovanni."

"I am the fastest boy at the stables," he declared in closing, then reinforced his point with a noisy, headlong descent.

After a moment, Carolina followed him.

"Your young friend distrusts me," Turri said when she reached the first landing. "Children are excellent judges of character."

174

For a moment, the impression of him standing at the bottom of the stairs, his blue eyes so bright they seemed lit from within, was so strong that she was surprised when the moment passed to find herself still blind. The vision had stopped her halfway down the stairs. Over the weeks since the Rossi party, she had imagined meeting him a thousand times, always in a haze in which the whole world fell away as soon as he touched her hand or spoke her name. But the actual sound of his voice had the opposite effect: instead of leading her into a dream, it returned her to herself. Her spirit, which had grown used to roaming fretfully between shadow and memories, settled back into her chest.

"I thought you were an old man," she said, and began to descend again. "With a cello."

"My worries age me every day," Turri said. "But so far none of them have resulted in music."

Carolina came down the final step. Turri kissed the side of her face. Something sharp dug into the bodice of her dress. She pulled away.

Turri laughed. "You have discovered your present," he said.

"You brought me a pony," Carolina guessed.

"A very small pony," Turri conceded. "With sticks for legs. If you'll sit down, I'll make him dance."

With an even step, Carolina led him into the conservatory, but when she turned to take a seat on the divan, he caught her hand. For a few breaths, he held it tight, like a giddy man catching at the limb of a tree to regain his balance. Then he released her.

"No," he said. "Sit at that little desk."

Carolina crossed to the desk. Turri followed close. The instant her hand rested on the back of the chair, he pulled it out for her. Dutifully, she sat.

"Now," Turri said, his voice strange with excitement. "A moment."

The coarse fabric of his coat fell against her bare arm as he set something on the desk. Paper rustled and the faint, sharp smell of charcoal came and went. He turned some kind of gear, as if winding a clock, and the paper rattled and cracked.

"There," he said, and stepped back.

"Should I sing?" Carolina asked.

"Sing?" Turri repeated, surprised.

"How can he dance without any music?"

Turri laughed. Then he leaned over her chair so that his shoulders sheltered hers. His fingers brushed down her arms to her hands, which he caught in his and lifted.

176

When he released her fingers, they settled on the keys of a new machine.

Carolina shivered. "What is it?" she whispered.

"It's a writing machine," he answered, his voice low and gentle, as if not to spook a shy animal. "Look."

He covered her right hand with his own, and pressed her index finger down. The key below it gave way. Nearby, something hit the paper with a determined slap.

"That's a letter," he whispered.

"Which letter is it?" she whispered back.

"I," he said. He spread her fingers over two rows of keys. "There is one for each letter. All twenty-one," he said. "They are in order by the alphabet."

Carolina extracted her hands from his and ran her fingers over the unfamiliar keys. Turri's arms still encircled her from behind. Faint heat pulsed through his thin shirt and vest.

She struck another. "That is a letter?" she asked.

Turri nodded. His chin brushed her cheek.

"Don't tell me," she said. Leaving one finger on the key, she counted away from it, to the beginning of the row, and then counted back again. "G," she said.

"It works with two pages," Turri said.

"One is black paper, covered with soot. The key makes an impression through it to the next sheet."

"You carved the letters?" Carolina asked.

"No," Turri said. "I robbed them from a little press my father gave me years ago, when he still thought I might make something of myself."

"So it looks like a book?"

"Like a page torn out," Turri said.

After the G she had already struck, Carolina hit the R and the A in rapid succession. She had to hunt for a moment for the Z, followed quickly by the I and E.

Then she turned to face him, caught a handful of his jacket, and pulled at it. In a clumsy rush, he knelt on the floor beside her. For a long moment, the only sound she could hear was his breath. Then, gently, he turned her chin so that her lips could find his. In Carolina's mind, the roof above them swung open on a great hinge, exposing the room to the clear sky.

Turri was the first to pull away. One of Carolina's hands closed on the collar of his shirt, the other in the hair at the back of his neck. "No," she said.

"Carolina," Turri whispered. "Anyone can come in here."

This seemed impossible to Carolina. The

kiss had unmoored her. It was easier for her to believe that the room had put out to sea than that the daily operations of the house continued around them as always.

But as if to prove his warning, a door rattled down the hall and footsteps approached.

Turri kissed her cheek and stood. "Write to me," he said. "Tell me when you'll be at the lake."

"I can't get out," she told him. Looking up into darkness at a face she couldn't see, it felt like saying a prayer.

The footsteps stopped in the door.

"Good morning," Turri said.

Fabric whispered to itself as someone bowed or curtsied.

"May I bring you anything, Contessa?" a woman asked. Carolina recognized the voice as Dolce, one of the maids who served her dinners with Pietro.

"Oh, no," Turri said. "I was just about to go."

"Shall I show you out?" Dolce asked.

"Thank you," Turri said. He bent over Carolina and kissed her hand. "Write me," he said again. Then he crossed the room.

In the hall, a key clattered in the lock. Turri and Dolce exchanged thanks and good wishes. Then the door swung shut and the key rattled again. A moment later, Dolce returned to Carolina.

"Will there be anything else?" she asked.

"No, thank you, Dolce," Carolina said.

She listened, but Dolce didn't retreat. "What is it?" the old woman asked after a moment.

"It is a writing machine," Carolina answered.

"A writing machine?" Dolce repeated.

Carolina nodded.

"What does it do?" Dolce asked.

"It writes," Carolina said.

"That's all?"

Carolina nodded again.

Dolce made a sound in her throat, unimpressed but tolerant, as if one of the boys had brought her a basket of windfall fruit instead of bothering to climb up in the high branches for the best specimens. "The Holy Father has a philosopher's stone," she offered. "It turns water into gold."

"Can you sleep with your eyes open?" Pietro asked. He perched on the curved arm of the conservatory divan where Carolina nestled. She hadn't moved from the spot since Turri left, hours earlier. She'd spent the afternoon adrift with the memory of his kiss, which returned to her each time with a

180

new feeling: longing, desire, shame, and gratitude so deep she was afraid her heart might attract God's attention by giving thanks when she ought to be making confession. Most of the time, the moment seemed like a dream. When it began to seem too real, hope paralyzed her or fear filled up her lungs.

"No," she answered. For the first time since she had gone blind, she wished that she could see her husband's eyes. Instead, she closed her own.

Pietro smoothed her hair. "But why would that be," he said, "when the light can't wake you now?"

"I don't know," Carolina murmured.

"It's a question for science," Pietro concluded.

He kissed the top of her head and went to the piano, where he played a few disconnected notes, and finished with a strong but clumsy major chord.

"They tried to teach me music," he said, and laughed. "It was like teaching a dog to sing." He played the first bars of a famous waltz, then let the left hand drop away but marched through to the close of the melody.

"Your violin player is all right?" he asked as the last notes died.

At the mention of this small kindness,

181

Carolina's heart lurched like a boat struck by a swell. "He's wonderful," she said, and sat up. "Thank you."

"He's very ugly," Pietro told her. "But he plays as if no one can see him."

As he spoke, he left the piano, passed the ledge of marble that hung over the fireplace, then stopped at the desk where Turri had set his machine.

"What is this?" he asked.

"What?" Carolina said.

A key rattled unsteadily against paper.

"Look at that!" Pietro exclaimed. "It makes a letter!"

"It's a writing machine," Carolina said.

Another key struck, this time more forcefully.

"How do you know which letter is which?" Pietro said.

"They are in order by the alphabet."

"Aha!" Pietro said. A flurry of keystrokes followed. "I have spelled your name," he announced after an interval. "With one extra letter: *Casrolina.* Where did you get this?"

"Turri," Carolina said. "It is one of his experiments."

"Turri," Pietro repeated.

"This way I can write to my father," Carolina said. "Or to our friends. I tried to write before, but the ink went everywhere."

Another flurry of keystrokes. Then Pietro pushed the chair back, crossed the room to kiss her, and turned to go.

When he reached the door, she couldn't stand it any longer.

"What did you write?" she asked.

"You have to guess!" he answered, and laughed.

When Carolina awoke that night, someone stepped lightly away from the side of her bed. Even with the deafness of sleep still fading from her ears, she knew how close they had been: so near it could have been their touch that woke her. She threw back the covers and sprang to her feet, but the footsteps were already outside, paused at the head of the stairs. When Carolina crossed her own threshold, they hurried down.

She rushed after them along the curve of the staircase, through the hall, to the dining room. By the time she reached it, they were already on the far side. A few steps more and they could easily have lost her, darting into the kitchen or the pantry. Instead, they seemed to wait until she had almost reached them. Then they opened the door to the cellar and plunged in.

Carolina hesitated at the top of the cellar stairs, held back by old fear of the dark, but her months spent in full night had robbed the fear of its power. She caught the worn railing and followed it down. On the hard-packed dirt of the cellar floor below, the footsteps no longer creaked and echoed. They were reduced to a faint padding and an occasional scrape, still unmistakable in the silence.

The only time Carolina had ever opened the cellar door, the cook had chased her away, defending her territory with all the sound and fury of the fowl that ruled the corners of the yard. Carolina had assumed that the space must be a single room, perhaps mirroring the shape of the kitchen, but as she followed the scuffle and slap of the footsteps, the chambers beneath the house seemed to run on and on. Her hands brushed rough walls, a row of bottles, a table strewn with tools. She stumbled on the raised stone thresholds of at least three rooms.

She guessed they must have crossed below the dining room, gone under Pietro's office, and struck into the outer reaches of the house. As they pressed on, she began to wonder if perhaps they hadn't already passed beyond the mansion's foundations and entered some secret tunnel dug by one of Pietro's ancestors a hundred years ago to smuggle lovers or other valuables.

Then the footsteps stopped. An inhuman groan split the darkness.

Carolina froze, her hands clenched at her sides, her mind black with fear, until a cool summer breeze touched her face, carrying a faint trace of lemon. Some part of the cellar had opened to the yard.

Carolina stepped forward and reached out. Her fingers caught a vine. Following its trail led her up a shallow set of stone stairs into the back garden. The footsteps vanished in the soft grass, leaving no hint as to whether they meant this latest adventure as a trick or an escape.

It was a little of both. For the first time since she discovered the front door locked, Carolina was free of the house — but she didn't know if she could find her way back through the unfamiliar labyrinth of the cellar. The lure of freedom decided her. First she knelt to find the cellar door, which was set into the slope of the garden. She lifted it from the flowers it had fallen open on. With a brief shriek and a whimper, it dropped back into place. She yanked the old wood a few inches to make sure it would still swing free when she returned. It did.

The night was warm and in the heart of the garden the scent of lemon gave way to the heavy perfume of lilies, fainter rose, and mint. Carolina let her head drop back, remembering the stars.

Then she turned toward the house. She tramped a few steps through the invisible growth to the foundation. She laid one palm flat against the pebbled stucco, and then, using the house as a guide, she began to trace its outline, following the walls from the back garden, through the ancient lilacs that screened the side yard, to the front walk. She followed it out to the road, and darted across to the tall grass on the other side.

This was where she should have found the garden stakes that would lead her to her lake, but although she found the break in the grass where she had tramped out a path, she didn't find the twine or sticks. She covered about twenty paces, bent low to touch the tall grass that marked the path on either side, but then the grasses dropped away, leaving her in a clearing with no hint of what direction to take. Beyond the clearing was the pine forest, small enough to cross if she knew the way, but large enough to disappear in if she was lost.

Behind her, grass rustled.

Then it rustled again. Another time, and the footsteps were unmistakable.

Carolina whirled where she stood.

"Contessa!" Giovanni cried, his boy's voice high with the effort of controlling his fright. "Are you all right?"

Carolina laughed.

The footsteps stopped in the grass. "I didn't know it was you," Giovanni said, his pride wounded. "I thought it was a ghost, or a witch."

"Giovanni," Carolina said. "What are you doing out at this hour?"

The prospect of an intimate interview with the object of his young affection distracted Giovanni from asking her the same question. "I like to run at night," he said. "If I run during the day, they throw things, because none of them can catch me."

Carolina took a few experimental steps toward his voice. Giovanni hurried down, caught her elbow, and helped her back to the road at the crest of the hill.

"So you really are the fastest boy in the yard?" Carolina asked.

"That's what I told you!" Giovanni exclaimed, stung by her doubt.

"Of course you did," Carolina said, and added, to soothe him: "I never call for anyone else."

"You could call them," Giovanni said, feigning indifference, "if you didn't care how soon a thing got there."

Carolina crossed the dark road and stepped back onto the skirt of Pietro's lawn.

"How far do you run?" she asked.

"I don't know," Giovanni said. "Down the road and back. There are paths, in the forest."

Carolina laid a hand on his wiry shoulder.

"How do you go back to the house?" she asked.

Giovanni didn't even approach the front door. Instead, he led her diagonally across the lawn to the kitchen entry off the servants' yard. The door was unlocked. He pulled it open with one sure motion and led her into the kitchen, through the dining room, to the foot of the stairs. There, for the first time, he hesitated.

Carolina squeezed his shoulder, then released it to reach for the railing.

"Thank you, Giovanni," she said. "I can find my way from here."

Giovanni gave a sharp, involuntary sigh. "It was such a beautiful evening," he said wistfully.

The next morning, Carolina settled a single sheet of paper into the machine. Then she lifted a piece of Turri's black paper and deftly checked which side was which. One face of the thin onionskin was smooth, but the other was dusty with soot. She placed the sooty side down on top of the other page in the machine, and set her hands on the delicate keys.

My dear father, she began.

When she had finished, she pulled the pages from the machine, set the black paper aside, and pulled the bell that rang in the servants' quarters. Then she folded the letter into thirds and pushed it across the desk until it butted up against the foot of the candle Liza had brought her earlier. The letter in place, Carolina picked up the stick of sealing wax and ran it up the stalk of the candle until the wicks met and the wax burst into flame with a small gasp. She lowered the wax close to the lifted edge of the letter, pressed the edge down, and listened for the sound of falling drops. Once several fell, she blew the wick out, picked up the seal, and counted to ten before pressing its face into the warm wax.

"Yes?" Liza said from the door of Carolina's room.

"Cut some of the lilies by the cellar and the roses near the kitchen door," Carolina said. "And take them to my father with this." She held out the letter.

Liza retrieved it far more quickly than Carolina had thought she could, judging by the distance Carolina had guessed lay between them.

"Shall I send Giovanni?" Liza asked.

"No," Carolina said. "Send Giovanni to me."

She didn't hear a sound from Liza until a stair creaked halfway down the first flight.

Then Carolina turned back in her chair, picked up another sheet, replaced the black paper, and began a second letter.

Carolina had only taken a few breaths of the night air when Turri pulled her into the shadow of the white roses that had almost overgrown the kitchen door.

"There's a light on," he whispered.

"A light?" she said. "Where?"

In reply, he kissed her. Answering heat flashed through her so quickly that it made her dizzy.

"In the front of the house?" she whispered when he released her. "It's only Pietro in his room."

"It's not a lamp," Turri said. "More like a candle. In the back, the corner window."

Carolina thought for a moment. "I don't know," she said.

"I couldn't stand to wait at home, so I sat by your lake until midnight," Turri told her. "You have a perfect moon on the surface, and a pair of loons who smash it to pieces every time something frightens them."

This time Carolina kissed him. When she let go, he made a small sound of recognition in the back of his throat, as if he had just grasped the results of some long-running experiment.

"Take me there," she told him.

Turri shepherded her quickly across Pietro's lawn and into the pines, pulling her back when she took a false step, his clothes and skin breathing a spice she didn't recognize. Under his touch, Carolina's dreams seemed to overrun the boundaries of sleep. The night forest around them, which usually lived in her mind as black shadow and scraps of sky, had turned bright as day, the branches crowded with white blossoms one moment, ablaze the next with blue and orange flames. The stars beyond the branches struggled to find their balance, reeling crazily, some burning twice as bright as she'd ever seen, some flaring out.

"You know the way?" she asked, pausing to catch her breath.

Turri stopped beside her. He folded their

hands together over her belly and pressed his cheek against hers.

"I've been this way a hundred times," he said. "When I can't sleep I stand in the woods and watch your lights."

"But I don't use any lights," she said.

"I know," Turri answered.

When they reached her cottage, he settled her hand on the weathered railing and let her climb the steps alone. Inside, the familiar smell of the lake, faint smoke from the fireplace, all the mingled perfumes she had worn among the velvets as a child, brought tears to her eyes. She turned back, suddenly lonely for Turri's touch. But he had stopped somewhere and gone silent.

"Where are you?" she asked the darkness.

For a long moment, no one answered. Then a hand turned her face up to his. Shaking like a branch in the rain, he kissed her mouth, her ear, her eyes.

When she woke, Carolina knew immediately that she was at the lake house, but she had no memory of how she had gotten there. Slowly, the early hours of the night returned to her, but tangled with her dreams and in fragments so blurred by heat that they didn't seem real. Seeing her stir, Turri pulled velvet over her bare shoulder. She found his hand and folded it under her chin as if it were a favorite possession.

Then her eyes sprang open.

"Is it still dark?" she asked. "You have to take me back before dawn."

"But we've been here for days," Turri said. "There are already two armies camped on our doorstep."

Carolina listened: no birds yet, no militant locusts. She sat up. "I have to go back."

Turri twined her hair in his fingers. "What if you don't?" he said. "Let me take you to a Greek island instead. We'll get a house by the sea and live on figs."

Carolina knew the book he had chosen this dream from: a collection of drawings of daily life in the ancient world that had been one of her favorites among those he sent, because of the pure turquoise in the water-color oceans. For a moment, the image of the whitewashed house high on a cliff rose up, achingly sharp, but then it began to lose shape around the edges, like a paper model melting in the rain.

"I have to go," she said, and pushed the velvet away.

"He says he brought you some balm," Liza read. "But now he needs it for his experiments. He wants to know when you could send it back."

"Nothing else?" Carolina asked, sitting up in bed. Turri must have written her as soon as he reached home. It wasn't even noon yet.

"There are some lines of verse," Liza said.

Carolina turned this over in her mind. The unspoken bargain the two of them had struck regarding Liza's lapses in reporting the contents of Turri's books was a new problem now that Liza held a letter from Turri in her hands. Liza was not a stupid girl. She knew better than to distort the central contents. But Carolina couldn't be completely certain what she omitted or embellished.

"Read them to me," Carolina said.

Liza read,

> A little bird
> stole my heart
> and hung it in a tree

Carolina measured the lines and judged them original. "Thank you," she said.

"Shall I call Giovanni?" Liza asked.

"Yes," Carolina said. "And leave me the letter." She held out her hand. Liza seemed to deliberate for a moment, then complied.

When Carolina heard Liza's light step on

the stair outside, she settled the folded page in a drawer and turned to the writing machine. Quickly, she tapped out a time and meeting place. Giovanni mounted the steps with a great clatter as she blew out the sealing wick. He reached her room as she pressed the metal signet into the wax.

"Giovanni," she said, extending the new letter. "This is for Signor Turri. Can you read letters?"

"I can sing like an angel!" he answered.

This was how the first weeks of summer passed: nights that began when she met Turri in the servants' yard, warm days crowded with waking dreams that slipped seamlessly into sleep and back again. Turri took to discovering the secrets of her body with all the passion of a great explorer. His curiosity was endless and his concentration complete. It excluded everything. If she let him, he would begin with a stray kiss at the back of her neck as he guided her through the forest and end with the two of them tangled in the loamy pine needles beside the path. Every night was a new experiment. He unworked the buttons of her dress, pushed it from her shoulders, but stayed a step away, tracing her lips, her jaw, her breasts to see where she resonated, when

195

she drew a breath. When they lay curled together he covered her face with his hands, learning her features by touch as if he were the blind one. He returned to the same curves and hollows again and again, to hear her make the same sound, or, turning his hand, to discover something he'd missed. Pietro's touch had confused her with heat and surprised her with pleasure, but he had never studied her like this.

The price she paid was high. Since the blindness had erased her world, reconstructing the rooms around her in her imagination had been a constant struggle. Now, with her days and nights inverted, sleeping only in broken fits, it became impossible. A gust of wind turned to Turri's breath on her skin and suddenly the piano, the divan, the staircase that she had set so carefully in place, were knocked away by memories that left her in total darkness when they faded. Without constant vigilance, she forgot where certain trinkets stood, what tables she had asked the servants to move. Vases seemed to vanish in thin air. Chairs seemed to appear out of nowhere. The real world became just as unpredictable as her dreams had been.

Her dreams themselves deserted her. They had been her one refuge from the blindness, but now they came to her only in scraps and fragments, like her sleep. At best, they lasted just moments, and the moments were nightmarish. In one, she stood in a long hall of statues: each one was blind like her, but she was frozen just like them. In another, she rose in flight, but as soon as her feet left the ground, darkness rushed in and ate up the whole scene. The loss of the freedom she'd won in her dreams left her with nothing but disintegrating memories to furnish the rooms in her mind, and to fend off the fears and doubts that followed her now like a flock of hungry birds.

Turri used the word *love* and she returned it to him like a student repeating a lesson in a new language, but during the daylight hours it seemed like too slight a word to bear all its meanings: her childish hope in Pietro, the promises she had made the priest, her father's shy gifts, Turri's skin on hers and his extravagant schemes. The only thing she knew for certain was that her mind cleared and the fears scattered when she was with Turri. But she didn't know how to explain any of this to him. For his part, Turri was still in the thrall of the dream he'd stepped into when she first turned to kiss him, willing to take all risks, full of tender nonsense.

"I can see in my dreams," she began one night, a few weeks after he had given her the machine.

Turri had been tracing lines on her skin with a feather quill, but now he laid his palm flat on her breastbone. "What do you see?" he asked.

"The valley," she said. "Our houses. The lake."

"Do you see me?" Turri asked.

"I see you," Carolina said. "But we don't meet."

"You should speak to me," Turri said. "I'm sure I'm much smarter in your dreams. I should give you questions to pose to me in your sleep."

Somehow, the conversation had drifted from what she meant to say. His joke made her frown in frustration.

Turri's knuckles passed gently over her cheek, as if trying to brush the expression away. "What is it?" he asked.

"I don't dream anymore," Carolina told him in a rush. "I wake up and I don't know where I am." Her voice rose as she spoke, dissolving into tears. Surprised by them, she hid her face against his shoulder.

Turri stroked her hair in silence. Carolina held her breath, but she couldn't keep the tears from leaking onto his skin. When they passed, she lifted her face to kiss his neck.

"Well, then you could be anywhere," he said gently.

"I know," Carolina said. "I hate it."

"No," Turri said. "The rest of us can't help seeing where we are. But you can be wherever you want. Where are we now?"

"The lake house," she answered.

"No," he said. "Where do you want to be?"

He turned his head to kiss her temple. Carolina closed her eyes. A wave of sleep rolled over her and receded, leaving behind the fragments of a dream: a palace abandoned in the desert, the roof now rubble on the marble floor, the columns still intact. The memorized lines of the lake house she had constructed in her mind shivered, then vanished. In its place rose weathered marble walls. Someone had hung lengths of colored fabric above them to block the harsh desert sun.

"A palace in the sand," she said. "With scarves for a ceiling."

"There," Turri said. "See?"

"There is a man coming up the walk," Liza announced. The chair she had dragged out to the terrace earlier that afternoon scraped on the stone as she turned to get a better look. "An *old* man."

Carolina laughed, imagining Turri's yelp when she conveyed this insult. She turned her face toward the break in the line of oaks that any visitor must pass through to reach the house.

"Now he's stopped," Liza announced.

Carolina smiled, and waved.

"You shouldn't do that," Liza said. "He looks like he's seen a ghost."

Carolina grinned wider, enjoying the effect of her trick, and dropped her hand.

"Here he comes," Liza said. "He brought you flowers."

An instant later, faint footsteps sounded on the gravel, maybe a dozen yards away. Carolina knew the gait instantly.

"Father!" she exclaimed.

The footsteps stopped again.

"Ah," Liza said under her breath, as if she had just untangled some kind of knot.

Carolina rose and took several steps in the direction the footsteps had last sounded.

"Cara mia!" her father said. He swallowed her up in his embrace, his jacket rich with the smells of tobacco and lemon. The cool blooms of a bouquet pressed against the back of her neck, their stems diagonal between her shoulders. Her father didn't remember them until she began to struggle gently. Then he released her and pressed

the flowers into her hands.

"They are yellow and red," he said. "The best we have. I chose them by their scent."

"They're beautiful," Carolina said, from habit. Liza touched her elbow, and Carolina relinquished the bound stems. A moment later, the door to the house thudded closed.

"Will you sit?" Carolina asked.

"Of course!" her father said heartily, taking the chair where Liza had been. Carolina worried briefly if the maid's chair would be fine enough for her father, then realized that Liza had undoubtedly chosen herself the best one she could find. Carolina sank down on her divan, worrying another detail: her father was not an old man.

"I got your letter," her father said.

"I'm so glad," said Carolina.

"Where did Pietro ever find you such a wonderful machine?" her father asked.

"It wasn't Pietro," Carolina said. "Turri made it for me."

"Turri," her father repeated.

Carolina nodded. When her father didn't speak, she added: "I think he was sorry that I couldn't see."

Her father still didn't answer.

The heat of shame rose from Carolina's heart into her throat. Her chest tightened. She searched through the shadows that crowded into her mind, trying to think of another topic to turn to, but found nothing. Finally, she simply reached for him. Her guess was wild, but her father caught her hand and settled it between both of his on his knee.

"You must miss your lake," he said finally.

"I do," Carolina said.

"Shall I take you there?" he asked.

Her father held her hand as if she were still a little girl, with all her fingers pressed side by side like pastels in a box. He tramped along in the low brush beside the trail so that she could have the clear path. A few times he stumbled, or seemed to work for his breath, and Carolina worried about what Liza had said: if the strong, florid figure she remembered was being bowed to an old man. But there was no way to ask.

In broad daylight, with a good guide, reaching the lake took only minutes. Carolina could tell they were near it by the sound of the frogs and locusts, and the smell of fresh water. But when they emerged from the shade of the forest into the cleared land that surrounded the lake, her father stopped.

"Yes, look at this," he muttered.

"What?" she asked.

"Hello!" Turri called from the far bank. A

moment later, with less enthusiasm, a second "Hello!" followed. A child's voice — Antonio.

"Your friend is here," her father told her.

"And his son," she added.

Her father crooked his arm and lifted her hand. She threaded her arm through his and he led her around the bank without speaking.

"We have reared a crop of pollywogs," Turri called as they approached. "They've been growing in jars on Antonio's windowsills, living on oatmeal. Today we set them free."

A few feet from Turri's voice, Carolina's father halted. They stood near the forest that bordered the Turri land, on the opposite side of the lake from her cottage.

"They're almost frogs now," Antonio explained.

"Did you already let them go?" Carolina asked.

"Yes," Antonio said. "The little fish came around to look at them, but one of our tadpoles chased them off."

"Where are they now?" her father asked, genuinely curious.

Someone must have pointed, because her father leaned over the water. "Look at that!" he said.

Carolina tried to pull her arm from his so he could move more freely, but he straightened and drew her closer. "You've raised some very brave pollywogs," he told Antonio with great seriousness.

"They learned all their bravery from Antonio," Turri said.

"And your father has built my daughter a writing machine," Carolina's father added. "Did you help him make it?"

"I saw it," Antonio said, unimpressed. "I can make prettier letters by hand."

Turri laughed. "That's true," he said. "Antonio writes with all the flair of a great contessa."

"Well," Carolina's father said, "I have you to thank for my daughter's letters."

A brief silence fell. Carolina strained to hear, but she could catch no clue to what passed between them.

"I'm glad for that," Turri said, after a moment.

"There are flowers in the water," Antonio noted.

"They have their roots in the bottom of the lake," Turri said. "Like an anchor to hold a boat in its place."

"Would he like to pick one?" Carolina asked.

"I could take one to Mama," Antonio suggested.

"You're very thoughtful," said Carolina.

There was a small splash as Antonio pulled one of the lilies from among the rest. "It's very pretty," he said. "I think it may be the prettiest." He sounded worried by this. "Is it all right if I take it?"

"Of course," Carolina said. "You should bring your mother the best one you can find."

"Are you a friend of Mama's?" he asked.

"They were girls together," Turri said, when Carolina didn't answer.

"You mother was a very pretty little girl," Carolina's father said. "She used to steal my lemons and try to feed them to the horses. Have you ever seen a horse eat a lemon?"

Antonio listened in rapt silence.

"At Carolina's tenth birthday party, your mother gave a lemon to a horse who was waiting in the yard, and when he tasted it, he spit it so far it broke the window in our library."

Another boy might have laughed, but Antonio waited.

Carolina's father chuckled. "But no one could be angry with her," he said. "She was too pretty."

"She's still pretty," Antonio offered.

"That's right," Turri said, as if his son had looked to him for confirmation.

A hand seemed to close on Carolina's heart. The pang echoed through her body. She struggled to keep her face still. But almost immediately Turri must have extended his hand, because her father leaned away from her to shake it.

"We certainly didn't mean to interrupt your visit," Turri said. "We ought to be getting back now. Thank you."

"Thank you," Antonio repeated.

"You're very welcome," Carolina's father told the boy. "Come and explore anytime."

"Thank you," Antonio said again.

"Contessa," Turri said, in parting.

Carolina nodded.

Their footsteps faded on the soft grass.

"Would you like me to take you to the cottage?" her father asked.

Hot fear washed over Carolina. She had no idea how she and Turri had left the house or what evidence it might contain. She shook her head. "This is enough," she said.

Her father drew her closer. His hand covered hers. "There's so little I can do for you," he said.

Tears sprang to Carolina's eyes. She caught her breath but when she let it out the tears escaped down her face.

"No, no," her father said. He folded her into his arms as if settling the extended wing of a frightened bird back against its own chest. "And now I've made you cry," he said.

"An island," Carolina told Turri. "The sand is white and the moon is out."

As the summer wore on, Turri had developed the habit of asking her where they were each time they met. At the question, a vision always sprang up in her mind's eye: hidden waterfalls, new gardens, unknown shores. Perhaps lured by these imaginings, her dreams had begun to return as well. They still came to her in fragments, but they didn't wink out as soon as they began. In them, doors that had been locked now opened under her hand. When she rose in flight, it was over familiar lands. The flock of fears and doubts still interfered with her thoughts, but she had learned to keep them at bay by never letting her mind settle too long on certain topics. The result was not peace, but an uneasy truce under which she was barred from inspecting the corners of her heart for fear the darkness would rise up and strip her of her dreams again.

The island was an invention, but the

moonlight was real. Since she had gone blind, she'd suspected she could feel the faint weight of it on her skin on clear nights, and she felt it now, falling through the window of the lake house.

"I can feel the moon on my skin," she told Turri. "Like sunlight, but lighter."

"And it is cold, where the sun is hot?" he teased.

"No," Carolina said stubbornly, and laid a finger on her shoulder. "Here, see?"

"You're right!" Turri said, surprised. "Try again."

"Scientist," Carolina said, and touched her belly, high, just below her breast.

"How did you know that?" Turri asked.

"I can feel it!" Carolina insisted, and touched the hollow of her throat where the bones that supported her shoulders met.

This time, Turri kissed it.

"You know why they have invited us?" Pietro said.

Carolina laid down the heavy linen notepaper, which he had handed to her despite the fact that she couldn't read the message, and shook her head.

"They want a line from your machine," he told her. "All the ladies in the valley you've sent one to have been lording it over the ones you haven't. They're worth more this season than a dress from Milan."

Over the past weeks, Carolina had sent out a handful of thanks and greetings as politeness dictated, using the machine. None of them had seemed especially noteworthy to her. "Who have I sent them to?" she asked.

"To Princess Bianchi, in exchange for a box of oranges," Pietro began. "Alessa Puccini, regretting that you could not join her for a ride in the country. Ser Rossi, when he offered you a quartet for the afternoon."

"I already have your cellist," Carolina said.

"Princess Bianchi has actually pinned your reply to an arrangement of ivy on her mantel," Pietro said. "She thinks it's very Oriental."

Carolina had never heard a trace of bitterness in his voice before, and it didn't suit him. She rose and carried the invitation to where he stood. He lifted the paper from her hand. She curled her arm through his and laid her head on his shoulder. She had planned to speak, but when her face touched the fabric of his jacket, she simply closed her eyes.

"It's true," Turri told her later that night. "They've got bits of your writing displayed in every house you've sent it. You should be a poet."

"Do they really?" Carolina asked.

"Sometimes they set it up right on the mantel," he said. "The more tasteful ones only leave it scattered about where you can't help seeing."

"So are you a hero now?" Carolina asked.

"Of course not," Turri said. "Too many of them fell out of trees in my machines or had their eyebrows burned off when we were children. I'd need to save a life to be redeemed. And even then it would be: *Ah, Turri, he seems to have come out all right in spite of himself.* But Sophia is already clamoring for a machine of her own."

"And?"

"I reminded her she isn't blind," he said.

"What did she say?"

"She doesn't care," he said. "So I told her I forgot how to make it."

"Did she believe you?"

"Of course not," Turri said. "But maybe it's how we make our escape. We can go to the city, and I'll build writing machines."

Carolina was silent. She hated it when he spoke of the future. His jokes about it were forced, his hopes so simple and impossible they made her seasick. His fantasies never lit any dreams in her own mind. Instead, they snuffed out whatever paradise she'd imagined for them, and even threatened the real walls of the lake house.

"Would you like that?" he asked.

To keep him from speaking again, she kissed him.

"This is the book of palaces," Liza said.

A few weeks earlier, Liza had taken a new risk in her narration of Turri's books: she had invented not just new pages, but an entire new volume: *Famous Shipwrecks.*

That first time, Carolina had insisted on detailed descriptions of forty artist's renderings of the unlucky vessels. Liza had cheerfully doomed each of her new inventions to a bitter end: one run aground in soft sand, but pounded to pieces by a warm southern wind; one splintered on black rocks as three bolts of eerie lightning struck the shore; one turned turtle by the storm that sank it, so that it struck the bottom masts first, and balanced upside down on the ocean floor to the consternation of passing sea monsters; one set aflame by pirates while at full sail, which gave the effect, Liza related with her passion for simile, of a birthday cake sinking into the sea; one glassed in by the ice of an arctic storm, all her sailors frozen to death at their stations. One, perhaps a favorite, suffered only minor damage after grazing the peak of an underwater mountain, then drifted gently to its final resting place on a bed of white sand, where the current pulled its ragged sails taut again, just as if it were still sailing merrily along in true wind.

Now, several invented volumes later, Carolina had become more discriminating: she was liable to make Liza reel off four or five options before picking one. "No, not that," Carolina said. "What else is there?"

In turn, Liza had also become cagey. Carolina, she knew, never picked the first book she offered, so if Liza had a taste that day for jungles, or cloud formations, she mentioned them later in her list. "Drawings of clocks," she said. "A bird springs out of this one."

"Is that all?"

"Blackbirds," Liza said.

"A whole book of blackbirds?" Carolina asked.

"No," Liza said. "They're all different birds, but each one is black."

"Not today," Carolina said. "But maybe later this week."

Liza paused for a moment. Then, trying not to betray her own enthusiasm, she said: "Deserts."

This was what Carolina had been listening for. There was no use, she had discovered, in asking the girl to fabricate blackbirds if she had no taste for them. But each afternoon Liza came to her room with a new scheme, guarding it as carefully as a hearth maid guarded a young flame. If Carolina could guess it from among the others, their time together was far more rewarding. "Yes," she said. "That's good. What was on the first page?"

"The desert at night. The sand is blue and the sky is black. There are —"

She fell silent as a heavy tread mounted the stairs below. A moment later it reached the threshold of Carolina's open door. "Cover your eyes!" Pietro crowed, then laughed at his own joke.

Carolina turned to face him. She heard Liza shift in her seat.

Pietro stopped in the door, as if to get his bearings or catch his breath. Then he announced: "I have brought you a present!"

"Thank you," Carolina answered.

Pietro crossed the room. He stopped opposite Carolina, beside the chair where Liza sat. "What's this?" he said. "The same old book of maps?"

The book swung shut with a slap. Carolina hid a smile. "You may go," she told Liza.

213

Liza's skirts rustled as she rose, then receded through the door.

Metal scraped on polished wood as Pietro set something on the table beside Carolina's chair. Fabric whispered, then snapped like a flag in the breeze.

"Hello!" Pietro said. "Don't be afraid."

"Why should I be afraid?" Carolina asked.

Now he was whistling: fragments of a song they had sung as children when a game was over but someone was still missing, hidden in the woods or the far reaches of the house.

"You've already found me," Carolina reminded him.

"Shh!" he said.

At the break in Pietro's song, the low voice of a sleepy bird answered him with a kind of exasperated mumble, as if to ask if Pietro's business could possibly be more important than the dream he'd interrupted.

"There!" Pietro exclaimed. "You see!"

At this exclamation, the bird apparently gave some other indication of discontent, because Pietro immediately apologized to it, his voice full of real remorse. "I am sorry," he said. "You will forgive me."

The bird, inexorable, refused to sing again.

"Maybe if you speak to it," Pietro whispered to Carolina. "I think he believes I'm to blame for all the jostling he suffered in the carriage today."

"I don't think they sing at night," Carolina said softly. "Other birds don't."

"They do!" Pietro insisted. "Some do. What is that story — with the girl in the palace? The boy she loves comes to her window at night, but the king turns him into a nightingale. Then the nightingale sings," he said, triumphantly.

Fear tapped a cold finger on Carolina's heart.

"Is this a nightingale, then?" she asked.

"No," Pietro said, taking on a professorial tone as he began to recite the details he'd gleaned at purchase. "This bird is from Africa. The captain of a ship collected two dozen of them for himself, but when he returned to Italy his wife had ruined him with debts from wild living, so he had to sell them. They filled his whole cabin. He fed them by hand every night, but not all of them sang."

"Does he have a name?" Carolina asked.

"The mate didn't know," Pietro said. "He was selling them because the captain couldn't bear to. I thought it would be some music, when the old man isn't here. And birds don't need to be paid in gold, eh?" he said, turning affectionate as he tapped the cage. "Just some fruit and seeds."

"There's only one?" Carolina asked. "Will he be lonely?"

"He'll have you," Pietro said.

Carolina reached out. Her fingers brushed delicate wire. Something shuffled inside.

"What does he look like?" she asked.

"Like a sparrow, but with green bands on his wings," Pietro said. "He's not much to look at, but he was the best singer. I chose him with my eyes closed."

"A pirate ship?" Giovanni asked. The cage rattled faintly as he tapped on the wire. Inside the bird shuffled, in a huff.

"I don't know," Carolina said. "It very well might have been."

"My uncle is a pirate," Giovanni claimed, leaving the bird behind to lean on the arm of her chair. "I have his glass eye. When I was born, his parrot was bigger than me. That's when he gave my mother his eye. He didn't need it to see."

"Really?" Carolina asked.

"No!" Giovanni said emphatically. "He only used it to scare people."

"I'm sure it's scary," Carolina said.

"It's green," Giovanni said. "No white like in our eyes. They say it looks like —" He paused, for effect. *A piece of the sea.*

At this, the bird burst out into energetic

song, a celebration so intense that Giovanni left her side to investigate.

"What's his name?" he asked when the bird fell silent.

"What do you think?" Carolina asked him.

"Babolo?" Liza repeated. She lifted the two braids she had just completed from Carolina's neck, twisted them together expertly, and began to pin them in place.

"Apparently it is the name of a singing pirate," Carolina said.

"Giovanni knows as much about pirates as I do about building a cathedral," Liza said. Carolina smiled. Recently, on her imagined pages, Liza had been constructing a whole suite of architectural fantasies: sprawling Arabian mansions, lousy with minarets; churches that thrust so far into the heavens that they made specks of the men and women who passed over their thresholds.

The bird trilled with perfect expectation of obedience. When their two voices fell silent, he broke into a raucous, rising song that might as well have been laughter.

"Were you king?" Carolina asked him. "Of your little cabin? Of all the trees?"

In answer, the bird began another song. His voice was a pure, flutelike whistle, and his catalogue seemed vast: scraps of dirges and laments smashed side by side with triumphant marches, wedding hymns, and lovers' fantasies, all of which broke off just at the moment they threatened to become melody.

"Carolina," Pietro said. "A card for you."

The bird's singing had masked the sound of his steps as he entered her room. Surprised, Liza let the necklace she had been fastening at Carolina's neck slip through her hands. Carolina caught her breath, then released it slowly as Liza retrieved the jewelry from the folds of her dress.

The bird scolded for a moment, then lost interest.

"Who is it from?" Carolina asked.

"Turri," Pietro said.

Liza succeeded in fastening the necklace on the second try. Then, without asking leave, she turned away. At the door she hesitated, as if momentarily stymied by the problem of navigating around Pietro. Then her light footsteps descended the stairs.

Fear beat in Carolina's temples. "Read it to me," she said.

"He says he has been reviewing the movements of the stars. There were showers of meteors last evening, and he expects to see them again tonight, around one in the morning."

This struck Carolina as unforgivably careless. "Why would he write that to me?" she asked, genuinely annoyed.

"It's not as if you can see them," Pietro agreed.

Carolina shook her head at the unseen mirror and turned on the seat of her vanity to face her husband.

"I'm smiling," Pietro told her after a moment. "You are so beautiful." He crossed the room and bent to kiss her, disturbing the jewels at her neck.

"Turri is a madman," he said. "Don't let him bother you."

"Please," Turri said.

The heavy scent of the kitchen roses on the night air made it hard to think. Turri had caught her as soon as she slipped out the door. Now he lifted her feet off the ground and dragged her a few unsteady steps toward the forest.

"No!" Carolina whispered. "I only came down because it was too dangerous to have you lurking around the house all night, with the servants sleepwalking and God knows who else making their own patrols of the yard."

"Your servants sleepwalk?" Turri asked,

suddenly a scientist.

"I don't know!" Carolina said. "Somebody walks through the house at night."

"A ghost!" Turri exclaimed.

"I thought you were a man of reason."

"Reason believes the most obvious explanation," Turri said. "Something you can't see, roaming the house at night: a ghost, obviously."

"But I'm blind," Carolina said. "Someone else might see them."

"I'm not ready to relinquish ghosts, even to science," Turri said. "I still have some things I want to ask them." He kissed her forehead, renewed his grip on her waist, and pulled her off balance so that she stumbled a few steps farther in the general direction of the lake.

"*No!*" Carolina said. "It's impossible. I can't be gone every night. Someone will catch us."

"Then I'd *have* to take you away," Turri said.

Carolina sighed with impatience.

His next kiss was tender: an apology, or a promise.

Behind them, something crashed to the floor in the kitchen. His arms tightened like a vise around her and she buried her face against his chest. Just as quickly, they parted.

"What was that?" Turri demanded. He pushed her aside, to sweep past her into the house.

"You can't!" she whispered fiercely. She shoved him back into the kitchen yard, stepped inside, pulled the door shut between them and threw the bolt, leaving him in the darkness beyond. She could hear his feet scrape on the stone outside, but to her relief, he didn't knock.

She crossed the small room inside the yard door and stopped at the kitchen's threshold. Inside, nothing now broke the night silence. Carolina pointed her toe and described a brief arc just beyond the doorway. The ball of her bare foot caught the texture of fine grains: sugar, or salt. She knelt.

Sugar. She lifted her finger from her tongue, then swept her hands lightly over the tile in a wider circle. This time her hands caught a shard of pottery: about the size of her palm, and razor sharp. Depending on the size of the vessel that had broken, the floor between her and the rest of the house might be littered with dozens of other dangerous fragments.

She turned again toward the door to the yard. She knew Turri still stood on the other side: he was liable to wait there a whole hour, after he'd heard the last sound she made. But despite the danger before her, the prospect of Pietro discovering Turri in the house at this hour of the night frightened Carolina more. She took a deep, silent breath, and turned back to the kitchen.

The sugar seemed to have scattered from the left, as if someone had hurled it at the floor instead of simply dropping it. To her right, the grains were not as thick. Her arms thrown wide for balance, she crossed the room with long strides, carefully exploring each new step before putting her weight into it. If she brushed the rough edge of a piece of pottery, she quickly sidestepped. She only hoped that she wasn't leaving a trail of bloody prints from cuts by smaller shards she couldn't feel.

In the doorway to the dining room, she stopped, listened, and then set out again, moving quick and quiet. When she had almost reached the other side, she caught the sound of footsteps.

Carolina froze.

The footsteps strode toward her purposefully from the sitting room next door, making no attempt at concealment.

For the first time, Carolina ran from the sound. She ducked into the cellar and pulled the door shut behind her. Hidden on the stair, she held her breath. As she feared, the footsteps entered the dining room, where they paused for a moment as if surveying the territory. Then they crossed to the kitchen, hurried: giving chase or making an escape.

As soon as their sound faded, Carolina slipped out the cellar door again, ran lightly down the main hall, and flew up the stairs to her own room.

"Fifty white roses, from the kitchen bush," Giovanni announced. "Master sent the order, but I picked them all myself."

Carolina's heart choked, then began to race with fear. "What a job that must have been!" she said, sitting up in bed. "I hope the thorns didn't prick your hands."

"I cut all the thorns off them," Giovanni said stoutly. "See?"

When she turned her head, he brushed the bouquet over her cheek, clumsily but with enormous tenderness, like a boy still learning how to kiss.

"I'll put them on the table," he said. "Where you can reach."

"Thank you," she said. Her heart began to slow, but now her mind ran to catch up. "Is it a little late?" she asked. "Was there any trouble in the kitchen?"

"Someone took the cook's sugar jar," Giovanni said, emboldened by the intimacy. "So she had to open the bag she'd put away to take for herself."

Carolina smiled briefly at the fierce old woman's dilemma. Then reason set in and her smile faded.

"You don't have to tell Master," Giovanni said anxiously. "She doesn't steal much, just sugar and chocolate, and oranges in winter."

"But they didn't find it?" Carolina asked. "The sugar was gone?"

"Someone took it," Giovanni repeated. When she was silent, he confided: "I think it was the ghost."

At the word, her whole body turned cold. "The ghost?" she forced herself to murmur.

"You don't have to be afraid," Giovanni told her. "When I go after it, it always runs away."

"I don't see why Carolina wouldn't enjoy going out in a boat," Pietro said agreeably. "You don't need to see to swim."

"No one said anything about swimming," Contessa Rossi replied, unable to resist an imperious tone despite the fact that she had come to ask a favor. Her parties always marked the open and close of the summer season. This year, as fall set in, she'd conceived a final event that traveled over water. The idea was to embark at Pietro's river landing and float down the current to refreshments and music at Carolina's lake. Carolina's father had already agreed to the use of his property. Now the contessa just needed Pietro's blessing — and Carolina's cooperation for the pièce de résistance: invitations from Turri's machine.

"I don't know," Carolina said. "I hate to use it too often."

"Well, I've been to Turri," the contessa said. "A number of us have. I asked him his price and he asked for half our ancestral land. He told Marta Scarlatti he'd need six live pear trees, plated in gold. Sophia says it's because he can't remember how to do it again. So I'm afraid yours is the only one in the valley."

"How many boats do we have?" Pietro broke in. He sat beside Carolina on the divan. That afternoon, without precedent, he had taken to smoothing down the curls that fell over her shoulder as an idle game. With one stroke, a curl would lie flat under his palm, until he released the lock and it sprang back into a dark wave. The unfamiliar gesture worried her, but the action was also calming, like water breaking on sand.

"Perhaps a dozen," Contessa Rossi said. "The servants can row them back upstream after each group lands."

"Fine," Pietro said. "I'll provide the wine. All our servants can set and serve."

"Wonderful," said Contessa Rossi. "And as for the invitations, my dear, I don't want you to go to any trouble. If you'll just have the machine sent around, I'm sure I can learn to use it myself." Her attempt at warmth was grating, like a singer reaching for notes far beyond her range.

"That won't be necessary," Carolina told her.

Carolina didn't like walking through Pietro's house in her dreams. The replica in her mind was full of traps and secrets: she would cross the dining room to the kitchen door, step through it, and find herself back in the dining room again, or climb the stairs to find the second floor had disappeared and a flock of birds now rested, single file, on the narrow ledges formed by the walls of the rooms below. Closets were filled with clouds of black moths. Candles were liable to set fresh bouquets on fire. Handles turned round and round but never moved a latch. There was even a child who roamed, like her, from room to room: a little girl so pale that some days her lips seemed blue, with thick black hair that fell past the white apron tied at her waist. The child was always carrying something, a cup or a twig or book, and as soon as Carolina appeared, she always hurried to leave the room.

After Carolina had learned to fly, she made a habit of leaving the house as quickly as possible when she found herself in it — usually through the nearest window. In tonight's dream, the one by the foot of her bed was already open. She padded over to the low sill and crouched to climb out.

Dawn was breaking. The fading stars hung in unfamiliar patterns: the spoons and the hunter were gone, but she picked out a bird, wings lifted to land; a boat in full sail; a crouching man.

She stepped off the roof and soared over the yard. When she reached the forest, she dipped into the crowns of the trees, and came to rest on the crest of a small hill that had sprung up beside her lake.

Turri was already there, tying off a complicated web of red rope that held together a filigree of broad sheets of parchment in the general shape of wings. The wings were supported by a skeleton of sticks he had constructed on either side of a pair of ordinary armchairs, nailed down to a small wooden platform. Between them on the platform sat a bucket of lemons that looked as though they had been rolled in soot.

"What did you do to those poor lemons?" Carolina asked, stepping closer.

"Don't touch them!" Turri said. "They're full of gunpowder."

Carolina crossed her arms.

Turri circled his machine, rattling the parchment, flicking at the sticks, and tightening a few of the ropes. "They're fuel," he offered in explanation when he emerged again on the other side. "Are you ready?"

Carolina nodded. He indicated one of the chairs, and she sat down in it. Turri took the seat beside her, selected a lemon from the silver pail, and dropped it into an evil-smelling black tube positioned just behind his chair.

With a sound like distant thunder, the contraption lurched about three feet off the ground and hung there, shuddering. Turri looked at her with delight, then selected another pair of lemons and flung them down the tube. This gave their conveyance the courage it needed to make its break with gravity. It lifted them steadily into the sky, cresting over the tops of the trees in the time it took Carolina to take in and let out a single breath. Their valley spread out below them, the shadows of all the trees and buildings enormously long in the early light.

"Look at that!" Turri exclaimed. "Have you ever seen anything like it?"

Before Carolina could answer, the dark tube behind them coughed, then gagged. Turri quickly dropped another lemon into it, but an instant later the long-suffering yellow fruit shot back out again, in flames, and punched a hole the size of a man's fist in the unlucky parchment that arced over it. Their little platform rocked like a boat on a rough ocean. Turri twisted to drop another lemon into the tube. The machine groaned, then began to hum again. The platform steadied. He took her hand.

An enormous thunderclap exploded overhead, followed by what sounded like a hail of pebbles dropping onto the wings that supported them in the air. Then burning bits of rind began to fall through the parchment, which curled away from the heat of the flames as they grew in strength.

As they hurtled toward the earth, Turri kissed her, very gently, as if he didn't know whether he meant to wake her or not.

Turri kissed her again.

Carolina opened her eyes.

"There she is," Turri said gently. "What

have you been dreaming about?"

Carolina sighed and turned her head in the curve of his neck.

"You built me a flying machine," she said.

"I'm very resourceful in your dreams," said Turri. "Under no circumstances should you ever agree to leave the ground in anything I build in real life. Was it a success?"

Carolina only hesitated for a moment. "Yes," she told him. "It was shaped like a swan, with a walking deck and a captain's cabin, and it ran on lemons."

Turri laughed and kissed the side of her face. He stroked her hair.

"It didn't work, did it?" he asked.

"No," she said.

"Here we are," Turri whispered when they reached the kitchen garden. "This is the door."

"I know," Carolina whispered back.

"You don't," Turri said. "I could have brought you to the gate of some fantastic palace."

"No," Carolina insisted. "I can smell the roses, and the knob always rattles in my hand." The latch came free now with a gentle clank. She pulled away from his final kiss and slipped in.

As she always did, she paused one step past the threshold, leaned back against the door, and listened, just like another woman might have waited for her eyes to begin to pick shapes out of the darkness. The house was silent. The scents of garlic and coffee still lingered in the air from dinner. She crossed through the small room to the kitchen.

From here, as long as she didn't panic, she was safe. There was no reason that she, as the lady of the house, shouldn't have wandered down for a cake or something to drink. She steadied herself against the door frame and bent to remove her telltale damp shoes. Then she glided quickly across the kitchen and paused on the verge of the dining room.

Outside in the yard, a dove cooed sleepily, which meant that Turri had been wrong, or had lied to her, about how close they'd come to morning. She struck out across the dining room, caressing the backs of the chairs that told her the way, and ducked into the hall.

At the far end, by the front door, someone took a step and stopped.

Carolina buried her shoes in the folds of her skirt and froze.

"Carolina?" Pietro asked after a moment,

startled. "Are you all right?"

Carolina's hand flew to the throat of her dress. With relief, she found she had remembered to fasten it. "You frightened me!" she said.

Pietro laughed. "You don't have to be afraid of bandits in our valley," he said. "All they could steal are books and lemons."

Slowly, with none of her usual sure-footedness, Carolina made her way down the hall toward him. Each step she took felt like a risk, as if the sound of his voice had torn holes in the unseen walls, or opened up new gaps in the floor.

When she reached him, he kissed the side of her face tenderly. "You couldn't sleep?"

Carolina wondered how much light had broken through the tall, narrow windows that flanked the door, and if it was enough to betray her bare feet.

"It doesn't matter when I sleep," she told him. "Sometimes I like to walk around the house when no one can see me."

"Shall I take you to your room?" he asked.

"Thank you," she said, her chest tight with fear. "I know where it is."

As she turned away, she swept her shoes over the folds of her dress and pressed them tight against her belly, so her slim back blocked them from his view as she climbed the stairs. It wasn't until she swung the door of her room shut behind her that she realized she hadn't asked him where he had been.

That afternoon, the cello seemed to be missing the home of its youth. It waxed eloquent about the long days it had spent wandering beloved roads, thought of the way light had glinted off the river that ran by its house, and remembered a chorus of familiar voices. Then it mourned, searching the streets of a new city for comfort, finding none.

When the song ended, Carolina lifted her head from the divan. She had never spoken with the old cellist before except to thank him or ask him to continue with another song, but now she wanted, suddenly, to talk with him as a friend. The desire to lay her burdens down at someone else's feet surprised her with its strength.

Almost as quickly, she realized how complete a stranger he was to her.

"I don't know where you come from," she said.

The old man was silent. The silence was so deep that the darkness in Carolina's mind began to eat up the walls and windows of the room. Involuntarily, she threw her hands out, searching for something to prove that vision wrong.

When the old man saw this, he answered, "Florence."

"Like the poets," Carolina said. Her hands had found the table of trinkets that sat beside the divan. She lifted a metal soldier from his place, explored the crisp lines of his uniform with her fingers, and put him back.

"Where did you learn to play these songs?" she asked.

The old man didn't reply. Carolina settled her hands in her lap and turned her gaze toward him, like a believer staring blindly through the screen at confession.

"Child," the old man said, "I don't want to know your secrets."

"The king is riding an elephant," Liza said. "That is like a cow, with a lion's mane."

She was narrating the life of an unnamed Caesar, told in illustrations. Liza was an able liar, but she was rarely inaccurate, sticking, with a liar's instinct, to topics she knew well, or ones that no one could know. Today, however, she was taking wild guesses.

"How frightening," Carolina said. She thought she caught a faint trace of a new scent in the room: lily and musk, some kind of perfume. When Liza turned the next page, the scent came to Carolina again.

"Now he has built a great tower out of sticks, and set it on fire. It's so hot that the sparks turn into stars."

"Liza," Carolina interrupted. "Is that perfume you're wearing?"

The book snapped shut. Liza said nothing.

Carolina laughed, delighted. "Is it a secret!" she said. "A present from a sweetheart?"

Stony silence answered her.

"Liza!" Carolina teased. "Are you having a romance?"

Fabric rustled, wafting the scent to Carolina again as Liza stood and dropped the book on her chair.

"Are we finished then?" Liza asked. "I am wanted in the kitchen."

"He seems to think we built this whole place just for him," Pietro said, bemused.

Babolo twittered for silence, then waited to make sure he had his audience's full attention before bursting into a song that Carolina had begun to recognize as his waking exultation. It was full of boasts, war stories, and rash promises, and Babolo reserved it exclusively for sunny mornings.

On gray days, he was apt to fall into reverie, with missed chances, distant shores, and unspoken love as his themes.

"I really think you brought me a little king," Carolina said. "Or at least the king's singer."

At the sound of her voice, Babolo broke off. He shuffled pointedly on his perch, his feelings extravagantly wounded.

"Oh, Babolo," Carolina said. "That was a compliment."

"Musicians are sensitive," Pietro said.

Carolina laughed.

Pietro had brought her an orange as a morning snack. Holding half of it in the palm of one hand, she traced the outlines of a single section, pulled it free from the others, and held it out to him. The touch of his fingers was warm on her hand, which had turned cold from the chilled fruit.

"And Liza!" she said. "Have you seen her in the yard with any of the boys? I teased her for having a sweetheart yesterday, and she stalked out of the room and won't come back."

Babolo trilled up and down a pair of scales, to remind them what they were missing.

"The cook even sent Giovanni up with breakfast," Carolina said. "Liza never lets him bring breakfast. I think it's because she steals half the fruit. There was twice as much this morning."

"Well, women are mysteries," Pietro said carefully. "Even when they're young."

"Yes, but you must watch for me," Carolina said. "In the kitchen, or the yard. She'll never tell me herself."

"I will," Pietro promised.

"Where are we?" Turri said.

They stood just inside the door of the lake house, slightly out of breath from the walk through the forest. Turri's head was bowed so that his forehead touched hers. His hands toyed with the clasp of the cloak at her neck. She understood the question: a request for her to invent another location in their ongoing game.

Turri kissed her. The lake house in her mind rose gently from its foundation and floated away into the sky. For a moment, shadows surrounded them. Then stone walls began to emerge from the darkness, glossy with mist. The two of them stood on a walk between pools of green water, under a low arched ceiling. The water was lit from below. Where the lights shone up through it, it glowed gold. The cloak slipped from her shoulders.

"A grotto," she said. "There are lights under the water."

Turri had been working down the buttons at the back of her neck, his fingers brushing the thin skin over her spine as he went. When he reached her waist, he unfastened the final clasp. The dress dropped to the floor. Turri's breath left him in a rush. For a long moment, he didn't touch her. Then he cupped her face in his hands and kissed her again. She searched for the skin beneath his shirt. One of his hands flattened over the wing of her shoulder blade, and pulled her to him.

Outside, a twig snapped in the dark.

The two of them froze.

"It's nothing," he said, speaking low. "Some animal. Listen."

This time it was not only a twig, but dry leaves crackling and shuffling as something walked through them, making no attempt to disguise its presence.

"The ghost," Carolina whispered.

"No," Turri said. "A dog, or a fawn." He stroked her hair gently, as if she were a worried child.

The sound from the woods stopped. Turri lifted her chin with his thumb. "See?" he said.

A step fell on the stairs of the house.

Carolina shrank against Turri, her bare skin cold with fear. The visitor hesitated for a moment, then ascended to the door. Turri crossed his arms behind Carolina's back as if bracing against a high wind.

It was a child's voice, thin with fright. "Papa?" he asked.

The next instant, Carolina was alone.

The door thudded shut and Turri's step sounded on the stair outside. "Antonio," he said, his own voice changed by fear. "What's the matter?"

Carolina crouched, searching the dusty floor for her dress. When she found a handful of lace, she pulled it close.

"I went to find Mama," Antonio said. "But she was gone."

Carolina could hear the stairs creak as Turri lifted Antonio in his arms. Still crouching, she scrambled into the dress. She managed to thread her arms through the sleeves, but when she tried to straighten, she discovered she was standing on the skirt, forcing her to bow.

"You weren't in the library or the laboratory," Antonio said, working through the possibilities with scientific precision.

"So you came here," Turri concluded. "That was very brave."

At this praise from his father, Antonio's

courage finally failed. "I was afraid!" he said. His voice rose and choked with tears.

"It's all right," Turri said. "All right. I'm going to take you home."

His familiar footsteps, heavy under Antonio's weight, descended the stairs.

Carolina untangled herself from her skirts and rose. For a few more moments, she could hear him passing through the grass. Then even that sound vanished.

Inexpertly, she fastened as many of the buttons of her dress as she could reach. She found her cloak and threw it over her shoulders. Darkness roiled at the windows and drank up whole swaths of the lake in her mind, but the prospect of being discovered by sunlight in the same place was even more frightening.

She slipped out of the house to the lake's edge, where she knew a few of the stakes she had planted the previous summer still stood, the twine she'd tied lax between them. Swiping at the reeds, she managed to find one stake that led her along a twisted string studded by broken wood to another stake still standing halfway down the bank. With countless false starts and missteps, she followed her half-ruined path around the lake and through the forest. When the strings and stakes ran out among the pines, she followed the rise of the hill to the road, then struck into the yard until she reached the stucco face of her home. She traced its walls back to the kitchen door and slipped through the house to her room. Her fingers clumsy with cold, she unfastened her dress and let it fall to the floor again. When she crawled into bed, the darkness consumed everything: the lake, the road, the house, her hands, stopping only at the threshold of her heart. For the first time, she welcomed it as it pulled her down into dreamless sleep.

"It's not much of a letter," Liza said, with a hint of derision.

Her knock had awoken Carolina only a few moments before. Carolina sat up in bed and pushed her hair away from her face. The room around her coalesced in her mind for a moment, flooded with morning light. Then it broke into pieces under an onslaught of memories: dark trees, black water, a frightened child. "Read it to me," she said.

"Forgive me," Liza read.

A moment passed. Carolina's heart swelled with tears. She bit them back.

"That's all?" she asked.

"There is a number," Liza said. "Underneath the name."

"What number?" Carolina said.

"One," Liza answered.

This was a time to meet, at one that next morning. "Thank you," Carolina said.

On the floor, Liza moved Carolina's discarded dress with her foot or her hand. "This needs cleaning," she said. "Shall I take it for you?"

"Please," Carolina said.

Carolina didn't choose to break the meeting with Turri. She simply knew, the same way she knew her own name or any other simple fact, that it was impossible to keep it. Some kind of veil had torn in her mind during the night, filling it with harsh light. In it, the lake became a searing flash. On its banks, Turri's form flickered, weak and thin, like a flame teased by a draft.

She tried to lose the afternoon in dreams, but sleep hovered just out of reach, turned skittish by the waves of shame that swamped her heart and the fear that roosted in her chest. Memories that she'd treasured of Turri, small jokes, certain touches, no longer worked to comfort her. At the same time, she didn't dare move. She had a sense that whatever had ripped the veil had also weakened her other defenses, and that now any slight motion might break open the locked rooms in her mind, releasing creatures she was still too frightened to name.

At ten that evening, sleep began to circle. To keep herself from drifting off before Turri arrived, Carolina set her anniversary clock to chime the quarter hours. The first time it did, Babolo was surprised. By eleven, he considered the clock an enemy. At midnight, exasperated by the clock's lack of respect for his vigorous protests, he fell into a grumpy sleep, determined not to dignify the strange machine with further attention, although he couldn't refrain from a few disgruntled notes each time it pealed.

Carolina lay on her bed as the hours fell away, her breathing shallow from the weight of fear on her rib cage. When one o'clock struck, her eyes were open, her hands flat on the velvet blanket. Over the hours, she had caught the sound of night birds taking refuge in the eaves, leaves shaking in the wind, the house creaking as the day's heat left it for the sky. But now there was no disturbance, inside or out. Somewhere, Turri waited silently in the shadows. When she didn't appear, he raised no alarm.

"Lavender," Liza said. "With green lace."

Carolina shook her head. It was an hour before Contessa Rossi's party, and a week

243

since Turri had left her at the lake. Every day since then he'd sent a new message: clumsily coded apologies, new times to meet. She hadn't answered any of them. This wasn't from new wisdom, or anger, or shame: her heart simply drew back from the thought of meeting him the way a hand recoils, unreasoning, from the heat of a flame. But as the days passed, the harsh light in her mind had dimmed. The familiar darkness rolled back in, carrying her dreams with it. She'd sunk into them gratefully, but with a lingering sense of dread that prevented her from flight or exploration. Her wishes had become simple. Often, she settled down wherever she found herself in a dream, to watch clouds slide over the face of the moon or water pass under a bridge, content to be any place that was not a nightmare or her waking life.

Turri didn't appear in the dreams, but by day she had begun to miss him, not with the desire that had drawn her through the dark house in their early days, but the way a tired child misses his bed. She knew he would be among the guests tonight. As always, she couldn't imagine a future with him in it, not even where they might meet that evening, or what either of them might say. On these points, her mind was a perfect blank, as if she had walked up to a white wall that stretched endlessly in both directions. But her heart hummed and her skin was alive with anticipation.

"A midnight blue," Liza said. "Black ribbons."

"No," Carolina said.

"Red velvet, with blue trim."

"That's a winter dress."

Liza shuffled through the depths of the closet.

"Blue watered silk," she said.

When Carolina didn't answer, she tried again. "Turquoise with navy trim."

"Are they all blue?" Carolina asked, half as a joke, half to hear Liza's retort.

To Carolina's surprise, Liza refused to be provoked.

"White lace," she said. "With light blue trim."

"The sleeves are short?" Carolina asked. "Just bits of lace?"

"And lace at the neck," Liza said. "With the blue trim around it."

"Bring it to me," Carolina said.

Obediently, Liza laid the dress over Carolina's knees, the bodice in her lap and the wide skirts spilling onto the floor. Carolina fingered the stiff lace, following its curve around the bodice to the covered buttons at the back of the neck.

"All right," she said.

Liza lifted the dress from her lap. Carolina stood and let her robe fall onto the chair.

"Here," Liza said. She rustled the gown on the floor in front of Carolina. Carolina marked its place with her foot, then stepped onto the swath of exposed carpet between the folds of fabric. When Carolina had her footing, Liza raised the dress and guided Carolina's hands through the sleeves. Then she circled behind Carolina and began to fasten the long row of buttons.

Carolina ran her hands down into the folds of silk that fell from her hips. "It still fits," she said.

Liza didn't answer until she had fastened the last button. "There," she said.

"I'll need some flowers for my hair," Carolina said. "But not very many. I can pin them myself."

"There are some waiting," Liza said. "Giovanni picked them this morning, but the cook wouldn't let him bring them up yet."

"Send him, then," Carolina said.

Instead of stalking off as she normally did, Liza lingered.

"Thank you," Carolina added after a moment, uneasy.

At the door, Liza stopped again. "Can I get you anything else?" she asked.

"That's all," Carolina said shortly, frowning in confusion.

Pietro had been at the lake all afternoon overseeing the preparations for Contessa Rossi's party, so it was Giovanni who led Carolina from the house, down the slope to the riverside. Dozens of voices already rose there: laughter and greetings and contradictory commands on the best procedure for launching the boats full of guests. Carolina strained to hear, her skin electric, but she didn't catch Turri's among them.

"I would be glad to stay with you," Giovanni said, gripping her hand proprietarily as they made their way down the slight incline. "You might want a glass of wine, or need to send a message."

"Thank you, Giovanni," she said. "I'm afraid they will take very good care of me."

"Now the master has seen us," Giovanni said, with a trace of resentment. "He will be here any minute."

The voices by the water dropped as she approached, until Carolina could tell she was only steps away from the crowd. She came to a stop. "You've been such a help," she said.

Giovanni squeezed her hand passionately before releasing it. "You look like an angel from heaven," he managed, as if giving up a military secret under some great threat.

"Carolina!" Pietro said, kissing the side of her face. "I have been in every one of these damned skiffs this afternoon. Your mother was convinced that we live too far inland to build boats that won't sink."

"Did any of them sink?"

"No, but I almost drowned the cook," Pietro said. "We had to put the musicians out to sea already. They were throwing sausage at them on land, as if it was some new kind of game." He noticed Giovanni, still standing by. "Well, all right," Pietro said. "You've delivered her. No need to stand there."

"Thank you," Carolina called after Giovanni's retreating footsteps.

"I am going to put you in line for a boat," Pietro said. "I would bring you to the front, but you don't want any of the ones we're loading now."

Out on the river, the musicians began to tune their instruments. Scraps of song flared up and then winked out again, lovely but incongruent, like a mural seen by the light of a single candle.

"Here we are," Pietro said after a few steps. "Can I bring you something? We have

248

lemon tarts and olives. No more sausages."

"Carolina," Turri said, and touched her arm lightly.

A thrill of fear ran through her whole body, chased quickly by heat.

"Hello," she said.

"Turri!" Pietro said heartily. "What do you think of our little party? Was it worth me soaking my feet?"

"I like it very much," Turri said. "The boats shaped like swans, the servant girls in wings."

"The boats are not shaped like swans," Pietro interrupted. "There is no need to tease her because she can't see."

"It's all right," Carolina said, and pressed his arm.

"A boat for Contessa," the servant announced from the water. "Sir, you will come, too?"

"No," Pietro said. "God only knows what will happen if I leave these creatures alone. This is a boat, not a swan, Turri. Do you think you can manage to get my wife safely to the lake?"

If Turri gave an answer, it wasn't spoken. He took Carolina's arm and led her down the bank.

Carolina settled back into the pillows in the

bow. Water lapped at the low hull.

For the benefit of the other guests on the open river, Turri began a neighborly patter. "This boat looks like it was constructed by the teenage son of the Rossis' gardener, based on Grandfather Rossi's cloudy memories of Venice," he said. "But I can't blame the boat. It even seems a bit sheepish, like dogs do when girls dress them up as children."

Carolina hadn't been able to imagine this meeting, but she had expected something ungovernable: a thunderclap, a disaster. To her surprise, she felt just as she always had, speaking with him a thousand other times.

"I never saw Venice," she said.

"It's a terrible city," Turri told her. He grunted with dissatisfaction at his own rowing. "A swamp, populated by the world's most stubborn gypsies."

Another stroke, and the boat glided forward.

"That's not what I've heard," said Carolina.

"They're not all gypsies," Turri amended. "Some of them are thieves."

Now the musicians had agreed on a tune: a popular dance from the last season. It carried clearly over the water, along with laughter and curses from other boats. On the water, Carolina could no longer gauge her location by the unreliable sound. One moment another boat seemed like it might be close enough to touch, and the next moment the same voices were barely audible.

"Where are we?" Carolina asked.

"Comfortably midstream," Turri said. "The real danger in a storm, as you're no doubt aware, is not weathering the open seas, but breaking up on shore."

Nearby, the broad blade of some oar struck water with a great splash, and then, encouraged by the satisfying squeals and shrieks, struck again.

"Carolina," Turri said, his voice low and changed. "I haven't slept for days."

"They can hear us," Carolina told him, trying to keep her own voice light.

"They're not listening," he insisted. "I can't survive it. You name a place. We'll leave the minute you say."

"Stop it," Carolina said.

Turri fell silent.

Carolina's heart felt twice its size. Her bare arms tingled as if threatening to turn into wings.

"Is it dark?" she asked.

"There are torches here and there," Turri said, with a hint of despair. "But they only make the shadows huge, and the water seem

251

like hellfire."

Carolina leaned forward, holding out her hands. When she found his, she pulled them to her face and kissed them.

"Turri," Carolina's father said curtly.

Her family's servants had dragged all the second-best furniture through the forest to the water's edge for the occasion. Carolina was curled into the corner of an uncomfortable couch, buried in thick quilts. Pietro sprawled beside her, one arm thrown loosely over her shoulders. Her mother and father flanked them in chairs on either side. The clearing was lit by torches on poles. One illuminated their small circle and warmed the back of Carolina's neck.

"Turri!" Pietro exclaimed. "Where have you been hiding?"

"He's been out in a half-swamped boat, trying to throw me overboard," Sophia said. "But he'd forgotten I can swim."

Pietro chuckled.

"You could hardly drown in this pond," Carolina's mother said. "A child could stand in the deepest part."

"It is nine feet deep now," Carolina's father said in defense of his creation. "Every year, the river carries away more silt. I dredge it each spring, when the ice melts."

"That's a respectable depth for any pond," Turri said.

"The first year, I had them begin digging even before spring," Carolina's father said, encouraged. "They were cutting up frozen sod while the snow was still falling. I made the men wash in the greenhouse each night, so my wife wouldn't catch on."

"But I knew," Carolina said.

"You did?" her father asked, surprised.

"I followed you," Carolina said. "And then I knew my way back."

"Carolina," Sophia said, "you must let me borrow my husband's machine. Everyone talks about it, but I have never seen it."

"Neither have I," Carolina said.

Turri laughed, then lapsed into the general silence. On the water, the musicians began to play a Spanish dance.

"It's such a strange present," Carolina's mother said. "What made you think of it?"

"You might as well ask him why he made a flying balloon out of my bridal linens," Sophia said.

"Did that work?" Pietro said. "I have always wanted to go up in a flying balloon."

"She wouldn't set foot in it," Turri said. "I sent Antonio up this summer."

"What did he see?" Pietro asked.

"He won't tell me," said Turri.

"Well, let him answer my question," Carolina's mother said. "Why a machine for writing?"

"Why do we think of anything?" Turri asked her.

"Yes, but a writing machine," Carolina's mother insisted. "You'd think you'd have made a device so she could see."

"I am a scientist," said Turri. "Not a saint."

"Here come the musicians," Pietro said. He leaned in to kiss Carolina, then stood. "I'm going to go and guard them from our friends."

The music had ended, and the raucous voices of the guests now seemed strange and out of place under the night sky. Peals of glee faded to low laughter, and the men's shouts died down to drunken mumbling, as if everyone had grown afraid of embarrassing themselves in front of the disapproving stars.

After Pietro had gone, Carolina pulled the quilt close around her shoulders, stood, and walked the few steps to the water's edge.

"I wouldn't do it," Turri said. "Real drowned girls are not as pretty as the ones they paint in pictures."

"How would you do it, then?" Carolina asked.

"I could put you in the balloon and cut the rope," he said. "You might get lost in space, or you might wind up on the moon."

"Did the party look nice?" she asked.

"You should have seen it," he said. "Pietro fitted all the boats with sails made from your servants' petticoats: turquoise, violet, green, and gold. Then he had lanterns hung from them, so the lake looked like it was filled with fireflies trying to escape from bags of colored paper. The musicians played on a floating dock inside a glowing red tent."

"He thinks of everything," Carolina said.

"He does," Turri said.

"There he is!" Sophia's voice rang out from farther down the bank.

Turri took Carolina's hand and kissed it, as tradition dictated. His lips on her skin were achingly familiar.

"Say the word, Carolina," he said. "Tell me when."

Carolina waited for almost an hour after Pietro returned her to her room that night. When she was certain that the house around her slept, she crept down the front stairs and through the front hall. In the dining room, she found one of the candelabras, followed the line of its stem up to the curve of its limbs, then fingered the gilt leaves that

255

clustered at the base of each taper. She dropped her hand to the linen cloth that ran the length of the buffet and traced the vines between its embroidered pears and grapes.

She passed into the sitting room, where she wandered among the scattered furniture, revisited favorite figurines, felt the brocade curtains that flanked the front windows. She crossed the hall to the conservatory, trailed her hand along the length of the divan, and touched the keys of a song she half remembered on the piano without actually striking them. She even walked boldly back down the hall to the dining room, where she opened the door to the cellar and took in several breaths of the stale air before she closed it again.

From time to time, she gave herself away deliberately, with a heavy footfall or the clatter of a china figure on the hard surface of some table. Each time she stopped to listen, but she never caught the sound of even a single footstep.

"That one was so sad," Pietro said, the following afternoon. Uncharacteristically, he had joined Carolina in the music room when he heard the old man playing. "Don't you have something more lively?"

In response, the old musician launched into a furious composition that raced from the top of his cello's range to the bottom, where it turned and skipped lightly back up the chords to a great height. It hung there for a moment, as if pausing to take in everything it could see from that vantage, then found a narrow path between the high rocks, and wandered thoughtfully along it.

"I'm not sure that's what I meant," Pietro muttered, shifting in discomfort on the divan beside Carolina. She had been curled up in the sweep of the divan's single wing before he came in, so all his bulk was balanced awkwardly on the tail of the couch, where her feet were meant to drape. At that point, the back of the couch dropped away, leaving him nothing to rest against.

"He doesn't like it when you call the music sad," Carolina whispered.

When the song drew to a close, Pietro rose, applauding loudly. "Bravo! Bravo!" he said. "Beautiful! I think we are done for this afternoon. Thank you!"

Carolina sat up, frowned, and waited for the sound of Pietro's footsteps to leave the room so that she could tell the old man to continue. But Pietro remained rooted beside the divan. After a moment, the old man's chair slid along the wood. His instrument thumped hollowly as he began to pack away his things.

"But he only played two songs," Carolina protested. "I listen for hours."

Pietro didn't answer.

Fear pricked the back of Carolina's neck. She folded her hands in her lap.

The old man swept his music from the stand. His bow clattered in the lid of the case. The fasteners snapped shut. Then he began to turn it on its end.

"Here, let me —" Pietro began, alarmed. Then: "Well, look at that!" He laughed. "I wouldn't have known you had that in you, old man!"

"Good afternoon to you both," the old musician said, and rolled his instrument from the room.

Pietro reclaimed his awkward seat at the foot of the divan and took Carolina's hand. He didn't speak.

Blood rushed from all corners of Carolina's body to her heart, which sent it flying back out again. Her chest and face burned. Her hands were frozen. "Pietro —" she began.

"No!" he said, his voice thick with some deep emotion.

Carolina sank into silence.

Pietro collected her other hand, pressed

her palms together, and cupped them both gently in his own, like a boy trying to carry a captured butterfly home.

"Carolina," he said, as quietly as she had ever heard him speak. "I have not been true to you."

"True?" she repeated.

"Faithful," he said, his voice rising slightly, as if surprised by the sound of the words he must use to confess. "I have — with Liza," he finished.

Carolina's mind made several false starts. Then darkness began to pour into the room from every window, sweeping away the tables, the rugs, the piano. She took her hands from his.

"How dare you?" she said, very low.

"I thought you knew," Pietro said, as if trying to work out a math problem aloud. "You caught me in the hall that night. And you asked me about the perfume I gave to her."

When Carolina didn't speak, he plunged on. "She's just a girl," he said. "A foolish thing."

"I know what kind of girl she is!" Carolina said, rising.

Pietro bowed his head against her belly. "I'm sorry," he said, his voice breaking.

Carolina lifted his face to meet the gaze of

her blind eyes. Whatever the effect was, it startled him to silence.

"Would you have told me this if I could see?" she asked.

His chin turned in her hand. She held his face steady.

"I am your wife, not your priest," she said. "I don't want your pity."

She walked precisely through the maze of furniture, out of the room.

Upstairs, she didn't hesitate.

She rang immediately for a servant. Then she went to Turri's machine and tapped out a message: *I'll leave with you tonight.* Below, she set the time and place, two in the morning, the lake house.

"Here I am," Giovanni said.

Carolina pulled the paper from the writing machine and folded it.

"You will take this to Signor Turri at once," she said, extending it to him. "If you have any other tasks, make another boy do them."

"I will be back before they know I am gone," Giovanni promised.

"Good," Carolina said. "Thank you."

Still, Giovanni hesitated. "But you haven't sealed it," he said.

"That doesn't matter now," she told him.

■ ■ ■ ■

She waited out the day in a seat by the
window, her heart numb and her mind gone
still, not through any effort of her own, but
like a machine stopped by a shock. Still, her
remaining senses worked. She heard the anniversary clock measure each fraction of the
hours, and when it chimed twelve, she rose,
found her cloak, and fastened it at her
throat.

As she passed, she brushed her fingers
over the double rows of keys on Turri's
machine. They were cool to the touch, as if
the moon's light actually leached heat from
them, instead of warming them like the sun.
The machine contained no paper, but she
tapped a few stray letters on the familiar
keys. Then she turned and went out.

The footsteps must have been waiting
outside her door.

Halfway down the stairs, they started after
her, following close. At the foot of the
staircase, instead of crossing to the door,
Carolina doubled back down the long hall.
The footsteps followed, along with the faintest trace of perfume.

Carolina whirled where she stood.

"Liza," she said.

261

The footsteps stopped.

Carolina lunged forward and caught a slim arm and a handful of hair. She loosed the hair, caught the other arm, and shook the girl, hard.

"You've followed me like a thief since I came to this house," she whispered fiercely.

"I wanted to see where you went," Liza said. Raised in pleading, her voice sounded like a child's.

"You left me out in the yard with no way to get back."

"You wanted to go out, but the door was locked," Liza said. "I saw you try it."

"So you are just a good servant, day or night?" Carolina asked.

"I don't know," Liza said, her voice breaking.

Carolina released her grip and pushed past Liza to the door.

"Where are you going?" Liza whispered, frightened.

Carolina found the knob. This time, it turned under her hand. She stepped out into the darkness.

For the first time since she had gone blind, she ran.

The landscape around her buckled in her mind. One moment, the house and trees stood just where they had always been. The next, stars glinted below her feet and strange mountains loomed in the distance. Somehow she descended the slope to the river's edge. Using the sound of the water as a guide, she made her way along the bank, catching at the reeds to keep her balance. This was the long way to go, but the only one that wouldn't leave her wandering in circles in the woods. They could pull up the stakes of the path she'd made, but they couldn't change the river's course to her lake.

Beyond Pietro's landing, the river grass leapt up to her waist and slashed at her hands. Carolina wrapped her smarting fists in the folds of her cloak and pressed on until the grass gave way to thorny scrub and untamed trees. Head down, she clambered through them, her coat yanking and tearing on the unseen branches. Finally the brush gave way to mud, and the mud began to curve in a long arc. She had reached the lake.

Hands extended, she made her way along the far bank, marking her progress between the trees. She found the twins by a lucky guess, took a heading from the way their trunks branched, and located the sapling just down the bank, then the thick oak beyond it. The apple tree led her on by the sweet smell of its rotting windfall. From there it was only a few steps into the branches of the willow that leaned over the bridge to her side of the lake. A moment later, she had found the railing: a slender limb that led her over the low rise of the dam where the river muttered under its breath as it collected itself after the drop from the lake.

Now she knew the way. Even as a child, she could have taken these last steps with her eyes closed. She followed the waterside reeds until she found the place where her father had rooted them out to create a landing. Then she turned and climbed the slight hill to her house. Her unconscious calculations were exact: when she reached for the railing that led up the steps, it was just where she guessed.

Inside, a short, angry sob escaped her. She let the cloak drop from her shoulders and kicked off her shoes. Her skirts were still heavy with mud and dew, but she curled into the cold blankets anyway. Darkness rolled in and took her under like a wave.

When she rose through the crowns of the trees, the light of the stars faded, as if someone had pulled a veil over her face.

Then they winked out. Carolina guessed that she must have flown into a night cloud and rose higher. Still no stars, no shadows.

Frightened, she dropped back toward earth. The descent seemed endless and the darkness absolute. Breathless, dizzy, she spread her hands out in hopes of catching a branch or leaf. Nothing but cold air slipped through her fingers. A new terror began to set in: that she might also be blind now in her dreams.

The instant this thought broke in her mind, she touched down on soft carpet. When she found her balance, she reached out in search of clues to the room she was in. She caught the beveled edge of a familiar table, found the anniversary clock just where she had left it, and leaned down to gather a handful of the covers on her own bed. Following its contour, she found the window and threw the curtains open.

But in this dream, as in her days, she could see nothing but darkness. She laid her palms flat on the glass, waiting for the dream to end and another to begin, but the ground held steady under her feet. She sank into a chair and bowed her head, pressing the heels of her hands into her useless eyes.

Green lightning cracked through the dark. Carolina caught the light and froze it in her mind with a fierce blend of memory and will. She had taught herself to move freely in her dreams, but she had never tried to change the dream itself. For several ragged breaths, she held the image captive. Then she glanced away from the lightning bolt to see what it illuminated. Outside her window, a cliff plunged down into a black ocean. White foam swirled around the foot of the rocks like punished ghosts. She let out a long sigh. Lightning cracked, and the scene vanished.

"No," Carolina said. She rose and beat on the window, tears running over her face. Her mind raced through the dark, throwing open doors, knocking over cabinets, searching for anything it ever remembered seeing. Then the lightning flashed again.

Carolina captured it before it even struck land, a jagged scar of silver light suspended over the black chimneys of a sleeping city. She narrowed her eyes at the incomplete bolt until it shimmered and broke. With one sweeping glance, she cast the bits of light across the eastern sky as stars. Thunder roared in her ears and lightning cut the sky again.

Her stars held steady over a ghostly desert. Another bolt charged down the night, but she caught it before it could turn the sand

to glass, broke it into pieces, and lit the
west. Thunder grumbled in the distance.
Miles away, a dark dune consumed a slender
tendril of lightning in perfect silence.
Carolina closed her eyes and erased the roll-
ing sand. She thought for a moment, and
opened them on the dip of Pietro's yard and
the old hills of Turri's land.

Then she decided it was time for dawn to
break, and the first rays of the sun slipped
over the familiar horizon.

When she woke again, it was morning. Birds
celebrated in the trees and a disoriented bee
buzzed from wall to wall inside the house.

Carolina frowned. Then she thought that
Turri must be there after all, watching her
sleep.

"Hello?" she said.

He didn't answer.

Carolina pushed the covers away and
made a quick investigation: the square of
rug by the couch, the desk littered with his
books, the chair, all empty. She stepped out
onto the top stair.

Some bird unleashed a long, gaudy call,
followed immediately by a chorus of taunts
and applause that fell away into the forest's
usual polite conversation: bits of news
passed between neighbors, morning greet-

ings, casual observations.

"Turri," she said.

The word bounced across the lake and died in the branches on the far shore.

Carolina stepped back into the house and let the door slam behind her. The cuts on her hands and arms, awakened by the motion, began to sting. She sank down on her couch.

Outside, footsteps swept through the wet grass outside and mounted the steps. The door swung open.

"Turri," Carolina said, rising.

"No," said Pietro.

The cook, who believed herself to be far more valuable than a simple maid, was insulted that she had been ordered to pack Carolina's things.

"They all look the same to me," she said. "I hardly know what to pick."

"Can you count to seven?" Pietro asked her. "Then count out seven of them. We will send later for the rest."

He had not spoken a word to Carolina as he guided her through the woods on the long walk back from the lake, and he didn't address her now. All afternoon she had heard shouts and confusion as preparations were made for some kind of journey. She had been too proud to ask the cook about his plans. But now she saw her chance to wring an answer from him in the woman's presence.

"We'll be gone more than a week?" she asked.

The cook interrupted her steady shuffling of fabric and paper to listen.

Pietro laid a hand on Carolina's face. His touch was just as gentle as it had ever been. It frightened Carolina more than his silence had.

"Tell her if there is anything you want," he said. "We are not coming back to the valley."

He kissed her forehead and went out. Carolina braced herself, expecting an onslaught of darkness, but the lines of her room remained sharp in her mind, the yard wide and bright, the sun clear in the sky.

The cook resumed her duties. She grumbled and hummed, stuffing silk and taffeta by the armload into the open trunk.

"That's thirteen," she said finally. "And I even fit four pairs of shoes, for all the good they'll do you."

"Thank you," Carolina said.

Babolo chirped his irritation with the uninvited guest.

"What's this?" the cook said, as if she'd

just discovered a mouse in her flour.

"What?" Carolina said.

A child's voice, one Carolina didn't know, answered from the door. "I have a message," the girl said. "For the contessa."

The cook slammed the cover of the trunk and thumped the latches shut. "Will you require anything else?" she said with elaborate politeness.

"No, thank you," Carolina said.

The cook trudged out, her tread heavy with displeasure.

"I'm sorry," the girl said, her voice wavering under the older woman's rebuff.

Carolina held out her hand. "No," she said. "Don't worry."

The girl placed the letter in it.

"Can you read?" Carolina asked her.

"Master Turri taught me," the girl said. "Shall I —"

Carolina laid the letter in her lap and covered it with both hands. She shook her head. "Thank you," she said. "That will be all."

Her step fairy light, the girl turned and left the room. Halfway down the stairs, the sound of her feet faded completely, as if she had suddenly taken flight.

Carolina turned the envelope over once, without curiosity. Whatever Turri promised

270

or explained, it was too late to change anything. The thought of him moved her only faintly, like a feeling from a dream that lingers for a few moments after waking. But despite the fact that she was wide awake, elements of her dreams filled her mind. The galaxies she'd created the night before appeared in the afternoon sky, white lights scattered through the even blue. She blinked, turned the afternoon to twilight, and reordered a handful of stars into a new constellation. Then she wiped the whole room away and replaced it with the familiar banks of her lake. It didn't matter where Pietro planned to take her. She could make her own world.

She laid the letter beside her on the bed and went to the chest. She unfastened the latches, pulled out the top dress, and let it fall to the floor. Then she collected the writing machine and the sheaf of black paper from her desk. She settled the machine on the top gown in the chest, and covered it again with the other dress.

Then she went down the stairs, leaving the letter unopened on her bed.

The horses shuffled, eager to be gone.

"Very good," Pietro told Giovanni, who had run from the stables to load their things

271

for them. "Someday you'll make a fine coachman."

"I can run faster than the old horses," Giovanni said, breathless.

"Careful there!" the coachman called.

Pietro left Carolina's side to rescue some last piece of luggage from Giovanni. A moment later, it landed on the roof of the carriage with a satisfying thud. "There we are," Pietro said. "That's all."

"Giovanni," Carolina called.

The boy scrambled to stand before her.

"I left Babolo in my room," she said. "I'm afraid he'll get lonely. Will you take care of him for me?"

Giovanni didn't reply.

"All right," Pietro said uncomfortably. "There's no need for tears."

Carolina held out her hand and Giovanni clasped it to his boy's chest. After a moment, she freed herself gently and stepped away.

Pietro led her to the carriage and helped her in. Then he climbed in beside her and put his arm out to rap on the door. The carriage rolled forward.

Carolina could feel them circle the yard, rattle down to the tree line, and turn onto the main road. She knew the dip down the hill and the rise to the next, where Turri's home gazed down on her father's orchards. She rode past the long boundary of Turri's property without turning her head, but when the carriage had climbed to the crest of the next hill, she closed her eyes and looked out the window.

The whole world she carried with her rolled out in her mind: the gold hills of the valley, dark lemon leaves reflecting the blue sky, and beyond them snow falling on desert sand, a boat cutting through the black ocean, men marching over autumn leaves, children fighting for their place in a parade, women who turned as one in a dance. Over it all, a small bird wheeled under the stars she had made, so high she knew that no one else in the world could see.

EPILOGUE

"What is it?" the man at the desk asked. His hair was as black as it had been when he was a boy, but all youth had left his eyes. The desk was strewn with schedules and bills and a selection of scientific instruments that would have made no sense to a scientific man: a decanter with a neck curved like a swan; a complicated sextant; a scale on which a gold ingot hung in an uneasy compromise with a handful of rough black stones that glinted in the firelight.

The man who had interrupted him was a stranger and a servant, in city clothes. "Signor Turri?" he asked. "Pellegrino Turri?"

"He was my father," the other man said, rising. "I'm Antonio."

"Pleased to meet you," the servant said. "I have a delivery for your father. A bequest."

"I'm afraid he's dead," Antonio said.

The servant raised his eyebrows, only

mildly surprised by the vagaries of chance. "Then I suppose it would go to you," he said. "You have a brother?"

"No," Antonio said.

"And you'll sign for it?"

Antonio nodded.

The servant crossed the room and set his package on the desk. It was the size of a stack of four or five books, wrapped in dirty fabric. "From the Contessa Carolina Fantoni," he said in what was unmistakably his official tone. "To be returned to Pellegrino Turri on her death." His voice turned confiding now. "It's been six weeks. It took the lawyer some time to find you."

"I've been here all my life," Antonio said.

"You know men in the city," the servant said. "They think everything outside the walls is wilderness." As he spoke, he untied the pair of knots that held the dingy cloth together. The rags fell away to reveal a small machine built of delicate dowels tipped with metal type, stained by sooty fingerprints.

"What do you suppose it is?" the servant asked.

"It's a writing machine," Antonio said, taking his seat again to face it more directly. "My father made it."

The servant touched one of the double rows of keys. A dowel sprang forward. He jerked his hand back. "What for?" he asked.

"So a blind woman could write letters," Antonio answered.

"The contessa!" the servant exclaimed. In the thrill of discovery, he reached for the machine again.

"You had something for me to sign?" Antonio said.

The servant dropped his hand to fumble in his pockets. After a moment, he produced a crumpled receipt. "That's right," he said, laying it on the desk beside the machine. He indicated the proper place with two fingers. "Right there," he said.

Antonio drew the paper to him, signed it without flourish, and passed it back. Then he opened a drawer, found a coin, and handed it to the servant. The servant grinned and turned to go.

"You knew her?" Antonio said.

The man turned back.

"Not to speak of, sir, no," he said. "But I knew her by sight. She lived in the city all her life, from the time she was married." These were clearly the only facts he knew for certain, but he hesitated, perhaps wondering if there might be gain in inventing more.

"Thank you," Antonio said.

The servant gave the machine a final look,

curiosity mixed with longing. Then he touched his hat and went out.

When the door had closed behind him, Antonio placed his palms on either side of the machine, as if checking for a heartbeat. He struck a few of the keys at random, and the print-tipped rods danced merrily. Then he lifted the machine from the desk, turned to the fire, and dropped it in.

It took longer than he would have guessed for the old wood to catch. For several long breaths, the machine stood intact amid the blue and yellow flame. Then the fire found it and the graceful shape was obscured by a riot of gold. After the first burst of fire receded, the delicate hammers continued to burn for several minutes, until the charred wood gave way and the glowing metal letters dropped through the grate and disappeared into white ash.

ACKNOWLEDGMENTS

Many thanks to Kate McKean for falling in love with the book; to Pamela Dorman for giving it a chance to see the light and to both her and Julie Miesionczek for their insight in the editing process; to Roseanne Serra, Carla Bolte, Beena Kamlani, and Sonya Cheuse for all their work in making the book a reality; to Alexandra and Daniel Nayeri for their close reading; to Teju Cole for giving the story its first public outing; to Kate Barrette for her translations from the Italian; to Ian King for his encouragement; and to Webb Younce for his kindness to a stranger. And to my family and friends, for everything.

The employees of Thorndike Press hope you have enjoyed this Large Print book. All our Thorndike, Wheeler, and Kennebec Large Print titles are designed for easy reading, and all our books are made to last. Other Thorndike Press Large Print books are available at your library, through selected bookstores, or directly from us.

For information about titles, please call:
  (800) 223-1244

or visit our Web site at:
  http://gale.cengage.com/thorndike

To share your comments, please write:
  Publisher
  Thorndike Press
  295 Kennedy Memorial Drive
  Waterville, ME 04901